Nothing but Ink

Also From Carrie Ann Ryan

Book 8.5: Inked Nights
Book 8.7: Second Chance Ink

Montgomery Ink: Colorado Springs
Book 1: Fallen Ink
Book 2: Restless Ink
Book 2.5: Ashes to Ink
Book 3: Jagged Ink
Book 3.5: Ink by Numbers

The Montgomery Ink: Boulder Series:
Book 1: Wrapped in Ink
Book 2: Sated in Ink
Book 3: Embraced in Ink
Book 4: Seduced in Ink
Book 4.5: Captured in Ink

The Gallagher Brothers Series:
Book 1: Love Restored
Book 2: Passion Restored
Book 3: Hope Restored

The Whiskey and Lies Series:
Book 1: Whiskey Secrets
Book 2: Whiskey Reveals
Book 3: Whiskey Undone

The Fractured Connections Series:
Book 1: Breaking Without You
Book 2: Shouldn't Have You
Book 3: Falling With You
Book 4: Taken With You

The Less Than Series:
Book 1: Breathless With Her
Book 2: Reckless With You
Book 3: Shameless With Him

Nothing but Ink

A Montgomery Ink: Fort Collins
Novella

By Carrie Ann Ryan

1001 DARK NIGHTS
PRESS

Nothing but Ink
A Montgomery Ink: Fort Collins Novella
By Carrie Ann Ryan

1001 Dark Nights

Copyright 2022 Carrie Ann Ryan
ISBN: 978-1-951812-88-1

Foreword: Copyright 2014 M. J. Rose

Published by 1001 Dark Nights Press, an imprint of Evil Eye Concepts, Incorporated

Sign up for the 1001 Dark Nights Newsletter
and be entered to win a Tiffany Key necklace.

There's a contest every month!

Go to www.1001DarkNights. com to subscribe.

**As a bonus, all subscribers can download
FIVE FREE exclusive books!**

Acknowledgments from the Author

This book has been years in the making and I'm honestly overwhelmed that I finally get to write Clay's romance.

Thank you, Erika, for asking about a certain honorary member of the Montgomery family so I could find a place for him in this big world of hope, love, and cheese!

To Chelle, Laura, Brandi, Charity, and Jaycee, thank you so much for being part of Team Carrie Ann and making sure this book shined.

I'm so honored to work with 1,001 Dark Nights and thrilled that they let me write a book where love is love is love is love and were SO excited about it! Thank you, Liz, Mj, and Jillian for being Team Clay and Riggs!

And thank you so much, dear readers, for joining me on this journey. I cannot wait for you to fall in love with these two as much as I do!

One Thousand and One Dark Nights

Once upon a time, in the future…

*I was a student fascinated with stories and learning.
I studied philosophy, poetry, history, the occult, and
the art and science of love and magic. I had a vast
library at my father's home and collected thousands
of volumes of fantastic tales.*

*I learned all about ancient races and bygone
times. About myths and legends and dreams of all
people through the millennium. And the more I read
the stronger my imagination grew until I discovered
that I was able to travel into the stories... to actually
become part of them.*

*I wish I could say that I listened to my teacher
and respected my gift, as I ought to have. If I had, I
would not be telling you this tale now.
But I was foolhardy and confused, showing off
with bravery.*

*One afternoon, curious about the myth of the
Arabian Nights, I traveled back to ancient Persia to
see for myself if it was true that every day Shahryar
(Persian: شهریار, "king") married a new virgin, and then
sent yesterday's wife to be beheaded. It was written
and I had read that by the time he met Scheherazade,
the vizier's daughter, he'd killed one thousand
women.*

Something went wrong with my efforts. I arrived in the midst of the story and somehow exchanged places with Scheherazade – a phenomena that had never occurred before and that still to this day, I cannot explain.

Now I am trapped in that ancient past. I have taken on Scheherazade's life and the only way I can protect myself and stay alive is to do what she did to protect herself and stay alive.

Every night the King calls for me and listens as I spin tales. And when the evening ends and dawn breaks, I stop at a point that leaves him breathless and yearning for more. And so the King spares my life for one more day, so that he might hear the rest of my dark tale.

As soon as I finish a story... I begin a new one... like the one that you, dear reader, have before you now.

Chapter 1

Riggs

I loved my bar, but sometimes I hated it. My bartender for the night had called in, a head cold that wouldn't go away. As I wasn't in the mood to help spread any germs or illnesses through anyone who entered the place, I was fine with them needing the night off. I just knew that meant I would have to work the late shift tonight. That was unless Rosie, my backup, actually made it in. She was trying to find childcare for the night to get in a few more hours. She'd recently been made a widow, having lost her husband in a car accident two months ago. I had done my best to ensure that she got as many hours as she could, and I'd even found her other childcare through some contacts I had. Only it didn't always work out, especially at the last minute.

There was only so much that any of us could do for one another, and I would never begrudge my staff for having to take off for being sick or for their kids. It all made complete sense to me.

Yet all I wanted was a night off like I'd planned. And I didn't think I would get it. That was fine. I loved Riggs'. I was the asshole who had jokingly named the place after myself because my grandma had liked it when we'd mentioned it in passing years before I even had the place. It had been a placeholder while we thought of other names. Then, I had run out of time to change it, so now people drank at Riggs', ate the damn good wings, and enjoyed themselves at one of the most popular bars in Fort Collins, Colorado.

However, I just wanted a freaking night off.

"We have two Keystones on tap, a honey lager, and an extra-dry martini."

I raised a brow. "That's a mix," I replied with a laugh as Kai, one of my servers, shook his head, putting the order in the system. When I was behind the bar and able, Kai liked to call out the drinks ahead of time, but we still keyed everything in since there was no way I could keep up.

At least, not tonight.

"They're an interesting crew. I think it's a double date or a first date. I'm not sure, but the two guys over there ordered the Keystones."

"What a waste of beer," I grumbled.

Kai snorted. "Unless you're playing beer pong. I mean, Keystone Light is the beer pong beer of the nation."

"Or at least of Fort Collins," I muttered, pulling the taps as I worked to make the extra-dry martini. We had happy hour specials on well for the night, which meant I would make a decent martini, but still, it wouldn't be as good as it would be with top-shelf liquor.

"Do you have time to make a frozen daiquiri with extra whipped cream?" Trudy asked as she came forward, her notepad in hand.

I held back an unprofessional groan. "Seriously?"

"And light on the rum. I'm pretty sure they just want a bowl of whipped cream, but they didn't want to ask for that," Trudy added with a laugh as she keyed in the order.

I went to work blending some ice and then made the next set of orders. Considering it was a weeknight, I was glad for the busy times. It meant that I would remain in the black this month and wouldn't go into massive debt with this bar. I still couldn't believe I owned it. It was all mine. I could pay my bills, and sometimes I even got days off. It was shocking.

I had gone through hell to get this place, to have it be mine where no one else could touch it. When I had first built the bar, I would have given it all back to have my life before everything changed. Now that I had been immersed in it for long enough to know the place and what it meant to me, I figured that, no, I wouldn't trade these past couple of years owning Riggs' to go back to a life that had almost broken me.

I sighed, pushing those thoughts out of my mind as I made up the next drinks.

Rosie walked in from the back as soon as I finished the whipped cream concoction, and I cursed under my breath. "Seriously? You show up *after* I'm done making the damn daiquiri?" I grunted, a small smile threatening to play on my lips.

She grinned. "You know I plan it like that. That way, *you* get to make them, and I don't have to."

"Sorry, babe, I have an order for four strawberry daiquiris," Kai replied, tapping his black notebook. "Our sexy bartender over here made them look so good, the new table wants them now."

I groaned as Trudy took the finished strawberry daiquiri away and looked over at the four women at the table next to Trudy's, who all waved at me, flirting as they looked over.

"Looks like Riggs has a new fan club," Kai teased.

"We all know that nothing's going to happen there since they're not a certain person," Rosie singsonged as she pulled out the second blender. "I've got these, boss. There's somebody near the back that asked for you. I didn't recognize them, but since they can see you, they know you're here."

All thoughts of their teasing fled my mind since I knew that whoever Rosie was talking about wouldn't be someone I wanted to see. It wouldn't be a Montgomery or one of their friends. Because if it had been, Trudy and Kai would have teased me even more.

I turned towards the back area and grimaced, my hands fisting at my sides. "You got this, Rosie?" I asked as she frowned.

"What's wrong?"

"It's nothing."

"Something's wrong. You're snarling."

I let out a breath. "Nothing's wrong. I just need to talk to this person. Thank you for coming in tonight. I take it you found a babysitter?"

Rosie tilted her head but nodded. "I did. And I want to thank you again for helping me get in touch with so many different people. I truly appreciate it."

"It's no problem, Rosie. We've got you. We're family." I hugged her absentmindedly and then braced myself for what I needed to do.

I looked around the rest of the bar, ensuring that even on a busy night like tonight, my staff could handle what was needed, and then I walked towards the man waiting for me.

Neil looked the same as always. Dark hair coiffed perfectly, the right amount of gel and product in it so it didn't look overdone but as if he had a two-hundred-dollar haircut. He wore a stone-gray suit that only highlighted the blue in his eyes. I knew it was bespoke with its clean lines. The man had a talented tailor.

Neil knew how to dress, and he definitely knew how to undress.

He also knew how to cheat, call someone a fuck boy, and try to take everything out of a person, including their bank account, heart, and whatever dignity they had left.

Only he did it with that growl of a voice and a charming smile.

I had been young, a teenager who'd thought he was an adult and, therefore, my world. He had put a ring on it, and I had been the dupe who'd gone along with everything the jerk wanted.

"What are you doing here?" I asked, doing my best not to cause a scene. It was my bar. Anyone who knew me—or didn't know me—didn't need to see me lose my cool. They didn't need to see me grumble and push and beat the crap out of the man who had never truly laid a finger on me but had taken nearly everything just the same.

"Really? That's how you're going to talk to me? It's been a while, Riggs. You look like you're doing...well."

It was the pause before *well* that made me want to slam my fist into his face. I wasn't going to be a violent man, I had never been, and I wasn't about to start now. I hated my ex-husband more than I should. I should probably hate myself more for making the decisions I did, but there was no taking it back. There was no doing anything when it came to Neil and his selfish ways.

"What are you doing here, Neil?" I asked once more.

"Can't a man just get a drink?"

"What did you call my place when I said I was going to build it? A countryfolk redneck bar in the middle of Colorado?"

"I may not be your perfect clientele, but you've done well for yourself."

Tension crawled up my spine as what he said hit home. "Too well?" I asked, knowing there had to be meaning beneath his words—there always was.

Neil just smiled, that pleasant one that didn't quite reach his eyes but also didn't go as far as if he wanted to take candy from a child. That strategic middle ground was always a bad sign. "Are you sure you want to do this out here where anyone can see? I mean, you've been doing well for yourself. It's so strange that things work out this way, don't you think?"

"Why don't you just say what you want to say?"

"I'd prefer privacy. Perhaps, you would, as well."

He gave me a pointed look, and I sighed before rubbing the back of my head. "Come on. My office is back here."

"I was sure you would see it my way."

I held back a grunt and let him follow me to my office. I didn't want him at my back. Didn't want him anywhere near me. The quicker I listened to his drivel, the quicker he would be gone and I could focus on cleaning him out of my system. Again.

"What is it?" I asked, not bothering to close the office door. He gave it a pointed look, and I shook my head. "Get on with it, Neil. Then you can leave."

"I just wanted to say I missed you."

I snorted. "Okay, that's a lie, you don't miss me. I thought you and Justin were doing just fine."

"Justin and I have an understanding."

"Nope. We're not doing this. If all you wanted to do was come here and pretend that you want me, then this conversation is beyond over. We're not doing that. You can go now."

"Come on, baby. You know you miss me."

"Nope. Not doing this. Out." I turned and pointed towards the door. "I'll remove you physically if I have to, but I wouldn't want to damage your suit."

"You'll be hearing from me soon. Don't worry. I'm sure you miss me."

Neil turned on his heel and left, smoothing out his suit as he did.

I crossed my eyes, then let out a deep breath. I didn't know why I let that man get to me.

He had nearly taken everything from me. And it had only been because of our prenup and my damn good lawyer that I hadn't lost my down payment for this place. Riggs' had been what my grandmother had wanted me to do before she died. And I had almost lost everything because my ex didn't just cheat on me, he cheated at everything else, too.

I bit back a sigh, pushing those thoughts away, and made my way back out front.

Rosie, Trudy, and Kai had handled the bar just fine, and people were crowding the dance floor. The rest of my staff was working, but it wasn't too busy anymore. The main rush was gone. When I turned, I saw a familiar group, some dancing, some not, though not everyone was there.

I only saw Annabelle and Jacob, along with Eliza and Beckett.

Considering there were usually more of the Montgomerys, a family that I had grown close to over the past few years, I was surprised that it was only the four of them.

I walked over after Rosie waved me off from the bar.

"Riggs! I'm glad you're here." Annabelle beamed as she squeezed my hand. She was heavily pregnant, and I found it hilarious that she still liked to come into my place, even though she couldn't have anything alcoholic.

"You're looking radiant as always."

"Be careful how you flirt with my wife," Jacob, Annabelle's husband, teased.

"Hey, I wouldn't poach. I promise. I'm a good boy."

Eliza snorted as her fiancé, Beckett Montgomery, laughed and leaned down to kiss the top of her head. "You may not poach, but I'm pretty sure you like the whole bad-boy image thing," she teased.

"Well, at least my reputation precedes me." I took a seat next to Annabelle and put her feet on my lap. Sitting on the other side of her and currently rubbing her shoulder, Jacob rolled his eyes but didn't seem to mind when I started rubbing her ankles.

"Oh, yes, right there," Annabelle muttered, and I snorted.

Jacob just sighed. "Please, continue to make loud sex sounds when another man rubs your feet."

"I will do what I have to, Jacob Queen. Don't take away my happiness." The teasing laughter in her voice made her big, bad husband give her a sappy grin.

"I'm just here to help the pregnant mama's ankles. Although aren't you due any minute now?" I asked.

Annabelle waved me off. "Stop it. Seriously."

I shook my head and looked around. "Where's the rest of you?" Although, it wasn't a Montgomery I was looking for, not that I would let them know *who* I wanted to see.

"At home or doing their own things." Something in Annabelle's tone concerned me, but I didn't say anything. They all had their own lives, issues, and worries. I wouldn't bother them by asking too much unless they wanted me to know. I'd slowly become their friend, but I was still their bartender—the pseudo-counselor who was there for a good time and maybe not a huge connection.

I frowned, wondering where that thought had come from.

"Anyway, we did bring our fifth wheel, as he likes to call himself," Beckett teased.

Eliza slapped his shoulder. "Be nice."

However, I couldn't focus on them too much. Because I turned and saw the person I wanted to see.

Clay Hollings.

The man I couldn't keep my eyes off of. The guy that I wasn't sure the Montgomerys knew I knew as well as I did. After all, I hadn't always been from Fort Collins. And neither had Clay.

Clay held a small tray of drinks and nearly stumbled as he looked at me.

"You know, I was going to say I should hire you, but if you're going to drop the drinks, I don't think you'd last long."

"You don't know how long I last, do you?" Clay asked and then blushed as he said it.

The Montgomerys whooped and hollered as I got up and took the tray from him. Our fingers brushed, and I watched the long lines of Clay's throat work as he swallowed.

"I have it."

"You're not working here. I am. Let me take care of you."

"I can take care of myself, Riggs. I always have."

I shook my head and moved out of the way so Clay could move past me. We handed off the beers and the virgin drinks for the girls, and I gestured to the dance floor.

"What do you say, Clay? Why don't you finally make me an honest man and give me a dance?"

I had been asking for a dance with Clay for months now. Over a year, if I were honest with myself. And each time, Clay said no because it was too much. Or he had to go home to the kids.

Clay had his own life and responsibilities.

And our tangled past didn't need to be part of his complicated future. Only after seeing Neil and watching my bar work the way it should—even short-staffed—I just wanted something that had nothing to do with who I used to be, and maybe focus on who I wanted to be with.

"Oh, just say yes," Eliza said as she sipped her drink. "Give us some entertainment."

"Am I not entertaining enough?" Beckett asked, his hand over his chest, clearly affronted.

"I love you, baby. But I want to see this dance of theirs happen."

"Do it, do it, do it!" the group quietly cheered, and I was grateful that the rest of the bar didn't chime in.

I held up my hand, and Clay sighed before knocking a shot of tequila back and putting his hand in mine.

"Fine. One dance. And then you stop asking."

"I can't promise anything."

Clay rolled his eyes and let go of my hand before we walked out onto the dance floor. The music was decently loud with a good rhythm, and people were dancing and enjoying themselves. We weren't a western country bar, but we weren't a techno bar, either. We were just your average neighborhood bar that played anything people wanted. Right now, it was a familiar pop song, one with a good beat so you could get close if you wanted to or dance in your little box solo.

I looked up at Clay's wide eyes, with his chestnut brown hair slowly falling in front of his face. I wanted to reach out like I once had and push it from his forehead, but I didn't. Instead, I just moved to the beat, both of our hips shaking, and I knew others were watching. Because I didn't go out on the dance floor like this. I worked. I worked my ass off.

Only here I was, dancing with the one man I shouldn't.

People surrounded us, and I was grateful that the Montgomerys couldn't see us from this vantage point. I moved forward and slid my finger along Clay's belt loops.

"I can't believe you finally said yes."

Clay sighed and traced his finger along my shoulder before he twisted, and we moved to the beat. "It's hard to say no to you, Riggs. Always has been."

"And yet you said yes tonight."

Clay met my gaze. "I don't always have time to say yes, Riggs. It's not about you, I promise."

Maybe it was because of the night. Perhaps it was because of what I couldn't have, but I blurted out, "Come home with me."

Clay blinked. "Seriously, just like that?"

I swallowed hard, my neck going red with embarrassment. "There's nothing quick about me wanting you, Clay. You know that."

Clay met my gaze, his eyes moving back and forth, and I didn't realize until it was almost too late that we were standing in a corner, hidden slightly by the wall, where no one could see us. Had he danced us over here? Or had I been the one to do it?

"The kids are at a babysitter's tonight. With the other Montgomerys in Denver."

I blinked. "Really?" I asked, knowing that Clay had his three cousins at home and was a single dad for all intents and purposes. He rarely had time off, let alone a night out. I hadn't expected him to say anything to my proposition other than "*hell no*" and "*go away*."

"I'm not closing the bar tonight. Rosie is."

"Okay, then." Clay leaned forward and bit down gently on my lip. I swallowed hard, wondering who the hell was propositioning whom here. "Just like before, then? No promises?" he asked.

I narrowed my gaze, knowing that my eyes had darkened, and my mouth had parted. "No promises."

Even as I said it, I had to wonder exactly what I meant by that.

Chapter 2

Clay

I should be wondering what the hell I was doing, yet I wasn't going to ask that question of myself. I wasn't going to question *this*. For once, I would think of myself and do what I wanted.

Damn the consequences.

"The number of thoughts running over your face right now could tell a story. Or maybe it's a whole novel," Riggs observed as he came to me with a glass in hand. I looked down at the golden liquid in the lowball glass, then up at him.

"Honey whiskey?"

"You know it."

Riggs sat next to me on his couch, and I let out a hushed breath, wondering how the hell I was here. I wasn't some young kid. I had been on dates before. I had slept with a man before.

It didn't mean that I knew what the fuck I was doing now, though.

"Cheers."

Riggs held up his glass, and I touched mine to his before taking a sip of my whiskey. The sweet taste slid over my tongue, and I swallowed, wondering if I should just toss the rest back.

"Don't you dare do it like a tequila shot," Riggs stated with a laugh.

I winced, then held back a laugh at what Riggs was referring to. The Montgomerys in Fort Collins loved their tequila and were damn good with it. "You know I like tequila as much as the next guy, but those Montgomerys sure can drink it."

Riggs snorted. "It's a little scary, to be honest. And none of them are assholes about it. They can do shots without lime or even making that weird face, and then let their designated driver or rideshare take them home. There's no fighting. There's no random backslapping or dancing on tabletops. They can handle their tequila. Just like I know you can handle your whiskey."

Riggs took another sip of his, and I did my best not to watch his throat work as he swallowed. It was hard to think with him right there.

With me right here.

He was so close, and I still couldn't believe I was here in his house. I wasn't at home dealing with homework, picking up backpacks or shoes, or tucking in a kid for the evening.

When was the last time I'd had an evening just for myself?

The fact that I had to ask that told me I should have thought about it long ago.

"Now you're thinking about the kids. I see the guilt all over your face. They are with Storm and Everly, right?" Riggs asked.

I nodded, taking another sip of the whiskey. "Yeah. Every once in a while, Everly kidnaps the kids and takes them to her house with their kids. They have a huge sleepover party despite the age differences between some of them, and I don't get a say."

Riggs nodded, a smile playing on his face. "If I remember right, aren't her oldest two technically siblings with your cousins?"

I winced. "Yes. My cousins share a father with the twins. Not that anyone outside of their dad and my aunt knew that until a couple of years ago."

Riggs shook his head. "I'm sorry. I didn't mean to bring it all up."

I shrugged, downing the rest of my glass. I set it on the table and let out a breath. "It's life. Honestly, it's old news at this point. It's been a couple of years, and the kids and I are figuring out a routine. Though as they get older, I think I'm spending more time in the car dropping them off at places than I am actually at home with them."

Riggs' lips twitched as he shook his head. "I still don't know how you do it."

"I'd say dark magic and alchemy, but I'm not a hundred percent sure how I do it, either."

"I'm glad you have the support system, though," Riggs added. "And I'm really happy you finally said yes to coming home with me." He winked as he said it, but something in his tone said he was hiding from something, just like I was. Or maybe, once again, I read too much into it.

I licked my lips, watching how his eyes followed the motion. "I figured it was time I did something for myself."

"As someone who is getting the better end of the deal here, I salute you." Riggs drained the rest of his drink and set the glass next to mine.

"I still think it's odd that the Montgomerys don't know that we know each other," I said, frowning.

Riggs moved closer to me then, his knee barely an inch from mine on the couch. We were facing each other, both sitting sideways. If I wanted to, I could reach out and brush my fingers across his jaw. I didn't, though. Not yet. I needed a minute. I had to remember how to do this part.

Riggs had danced with me, had his hands all over me, and yet, I needed to think. I wasn't good at thinking when it came to him.

"We were in high school," he said. "I still can't believe you let me kiss you back then."

I snorted, remembering. "We did a lot more than kiss."

"True. It's nice knowing that the guy you lost your virginity to isn't an all-around asshole, yet you're here and not a hot mess or a douche."

I laughed. I couldn't help it. "Yeah, well, I could say the same about you. I still don't know how we didn't get caught."

"Doing what we did behind the bleachers at the football field was probably an idiotic thing to do. However, it was nice under the moonlight."

"And trying to figure out exactly what the fuck we were doing that had nothing to do with porn was a blast. Wasn't that a memory?" I asked, laughing.

"True. Yet we got the job done."

My groin tightened as I thought about exactly how he had gotten that job done, and I sighed. "Eventually."

"I have better moves now. Just letting you know."

I snorted. "Good line there."

"Why don't the Montgomerys know that you and I slept together in high school?" Riggs asked.

I laughed. I couldn't help it. "Even though I brought it up, it's really an easy answer. It's because they don't know who I sleep with. I mean, the only reason I know who has slept with who out of that group is that they're all ending up married or having kids. Sometimes both."

"They're not going to have a problem with you and me? When they find out? Because they're smart. They're going to know."

I blinked, confused. "Nearly every Montgomery is queer, Riggs.

They're not going to have a problem with the fact that I'm bi. They know."

"I just wanted to be sure. They're your friends, your bosses. Your team. I don't want to be the asshole who fucks that up."

I bent forward and frowned. We were close then, so close I only needed to lean a bit more, and my lips would be on his. First, though, I needed to breathe.

"They're not going to have a problem with you, Riggs. *I* don't have a problem with you. The only reason I haven't done this before now is that I didn't have time. I seriously don't have the energy for anything but my kids and my job. Going to the bar like I do is once in a blue moon if the stars align—or any other metaphor and saying you want to add in."

Riggs tilted his head as he looked at me, his gaze moving to my lips. "Meaning, it's just tonight."

Something struck me then, a twist deep inside, but I told myself it was nothing. I couldn't feel remorse about this. Or guilt. I could just be. "It has to be, Riggs. I've got three kids at home. And a job I'm trying to grow with. I won't have much free time at all. Ever."

He reached out and traced his finger along the stubble on my jaw. "Okay, then. I don't mind being your distraction for the night."

That made me laugh softly, a chuckle rumbling in my throat. "You're always a distraction, Riggs. I think you like that."

His lips quirked into a smile, and then they were pressed to mine. All I could do was try not to hold back yet not give in too much. He tasted of whiskey and Riggs. Different than before, yet almost familiar. As if we were falling into who we had once been even while we weren't those people anymore. It was a memory, a ghost of the past, but then I wasn't thinking much about that.

All I could do was lean forward and tangle my tongue with his, gently exploring his mouth as he groaned.

"You taste damn good."

I looked up at him, gazed into those whiskey eyes after that whiskey taste. "I was thinking the same about you."

"You good with me continuing this?"

"I think if you don't keep kissing me and don't get your hands on me, I'm going to wonder why the hell I came over here tonight."

Riggs grinned. "I always knew you were the dominant one in this situation. Not just me."

I rolled my eyes and then leaned forward again, pressing his back to the couch as I deepened the kiss. He groaned, his hands moving from my shoulders to my waist. He squeezed lightly, the sensation hardening my cock even more.

"Get closer," he mumbled against my lips, and I moved to straddle him. I wasn't a small man, but neither was Riggs. His thighs were thick and hard with muscle. I wrapped my legs around him, kneeling as he sat me on top of him. We both groaned as I placed my ass over the hard line of his cock.

"Jesus," he grumbled against me. I grinned, needing more. I always fucking needed more when it came to him. And that was the problem. Had always been the issue.

Before, when we'd tried to figure out who we were to each other, things had ended easily because we'd needed it to *be*. After we parted ways, we'd gone to different schools, had different lives, and drifted apart. We hadn't fought. There was no big blow-up that ended things. It just hadn't happened.

Now, I was supposed to act as if this wasn't who we used to be? I pushed those thoughts from my mind, knowing that it wouldn't help anyone. I just needed to be—and I needed to remember that.

I pulled back as Riggs bit my lip, his eyes narrowing. "Your mind is somewhere it shouldn't be. Be with me."

"You make it difficult." I let out a rough chuckle.

"Maybe. It's just us right now. No one else. That might be hard. A hard idea. But we're fine. You and me. We'll figure it out."

I swallowed thickly, wondering why Riggs always did this to me. He had always been able to affect me this way. To make me feel as if I were losing my mind, even though he never pushed. He was just there. Always. Making me feel like I was the center of his universe, even for those brief moments.

He tugged on the bottom of my shirt as he kissed me again, then left a trail of kisses down my neck, biting gently on my skin. I groaned and lifted my hands, helping him strip off my shirt. I tugged on the hem of his T-shirt, and we both moved, the friction given the placement of my hips nearly sending me over the edge.

Riggs groaned, a smile playing on his lips. "Jesus. I'm going to come in my jeans. I didn't even do that when we were teenagers."

"I was just thinking the same thing," I whispered before sliding my hand down his body. He was all muscle but he wasn't bulky. I was thicker than he was, actually, from my days of manual labor that were a little different than a bartender's. Only I could tell that Riggs worked out.

"Swimming," Riggs said with a wink, his hands on my belt loop.

"What?" I asked, images of my tongue all over his chest and everywhere else filling my mind. I hadn't been paying attention.

"I could read your thoughts on your face. It's swimming. I use the Y every morning. That's why I look as sexy as I do."

He preened, and I threw my head back and laughed.

And then Riggs' mouth was on my nipple, and I groaned, sliding my hands through his long hair. It brushed his collar whenever he wore a shirt. Now, the strands slid over my skin, and I shivered, wanting more.

Then I was on my back. I wasn't sure how that had happened. Riggs settled between my legs, and he left gentle kisses all over my skin.

"I've missed this taste," he mumbled against me as he pressed his mouth to my stomach below my belly button.

"We're doing this, then?" I asked, looking down at him, the position nearly making me come right then and there.

"We'll stop whenever you want. But I will beg. Don't think I won't."

"Riggs, you never had to beg for me."

And that was the problem.

I licked my lips and ran my hands down my body so I could play with the ends of Riggs' hair. He grinned, kissed below my belly button again, and then worked on my belt. I lifted my hips as he slowly undid the button on my jeans and then pulled down the zipper.

We both groaned as he slid his hand into my boxer briefs and gripped me. The feel of his callused hand wrapped around my cock nearly sent me over the edge. He pulled me out, pumped me slightly, and then slid his thumb over the tip, spreading the fluid there.

"I think I forgot exactly what I used to do with this. I'd better practice." He winked as he said it, and I opened my mouth to say something snarky back to him. Only I couldn't think anymore. I groaned as he swallowed the tip of my dick, hollowing his mouth slightly as he started to work me.

I lifted my hips unconsciously, filling his mouth as he swallowed me whole, the tip of my cock reaching the back of his throat. And then he gulped, taking me deeper. I nearly came right then. I had to breathe through my mouth, panting as he continued working me, pulling me more out of my boxers as he cupped my balls, rolling them around in his hand.

When he hollowed his cheeks again and hummed along my length, I nearly came off the couch and pulled out of his mouth.

"Okay. Apparently, I'm a little trigger-happy," I said with a laugh, running my hands through my hair.

Riggs just grinned at me and shook his head. "I wasn't nearly done with you yet."

"I don't think it's fair that I don't have my hands on you."

"True." He looked around the living room and frowned. "Not enough room here. Come on," he said as he stood and held out his hand.

I swallowed hard and rose, pulling my pants up a bit so I didn't trip over them. I was still partially hanging out, and his eyes darkened as he looked down at me.

I slid my hand into his and let him drag me to the bedroom.

As soon as we entered the room, he pressed me against the wall—a little forcefully—and then dropped to his knees.

He sucked me down again, and I pulled at his hair, groaning. "I thought you said we needed more room so we could both play?"

"Sorry, you know me, blowjobs are my favorite thing."

"Really? I always thought you liked it when I played with your ass," I said with a laugh.

"Okay, blowjobs are *one* of my many favorite things. Now, get on the bed."

I shook my head and pulled him up, crushing my mouth to his. "No, first you're going to take off your pants, and I'm going to see if I remember exactly how big your dick is."

"You are so sweet. Were you this sweet before?"

"Shut up and get on the bed."

"Whatever you say, darling."

Riggs shook his head and slowly began walking to the bed, undoing his belt slowly as if doing a little striptease for me. I swallowed hard and shucked off my shoes and my jeans as quickly as I could.

Riggs did the same, no longer caring to play. And then my mouth was on his, and we were both falling onto the bed, our dicks pressed together as we clawed at each other, not trying for dominance, simply kissing and needing, each of us touching with gentle grazes and then harsher pulls.

He was so hot, and I couldn't breathe. I couldn't do anything but want his taste. Want him in me. *Want to be in him.*

When we were younger, we hadn't cared who topped. And I still didn't. I liked fucking. I liked being fucked. I wasn't sure if Riggs had changed in his preferences. And then he looked at me, my dick in his hand as mine was wrapped around his length, and we both groaned.

"Who wants to go first?" he asked, teasing.

"You saying you still don't mind?"

"I'll take you any way I can get you, Clay. You know that."

Something in his gaze told me that if we did this now, we wouldn't want to stop. Only I'd told him I didn't have the time. That I couldn't take anything for myself outside of this moment. I had to hope he understood that.

I nodded and kissed him again, afraid that I would say too much if I said anything. That had been another problem before. I always said too much. Wanted too much. And then I was disappointed when neither of us could provide it.

We adjusted ourselves in the bed, both of us leaning on our sides as I took him into my mouth, doing my best to swallow as much of him as I could. He was wider than I was, but I was longer, and we'd always joked that it had worked out perfectly in the end.

I hummed around his dick, wanting him to come down my throat, but also wanting him to come inside me. I wanted everything. But we only had tonight, so I had to be smart. I had to make sure I didn't take too much. That I didn't *want* too much.

I worked on him as he swallowed me down, both of us groaning as we bumped into each other's throats. When he slid his finger back, spreading me, I did the same to him.

We both froze, and Riggs let out a rough chuckle. "I think I'm going to need to be inside you. What do you say?"

I sat and pulled him towards me before kissing him hard. "I'm saying you'd better have fucking lube."

Riggs rolled his eyes. "What do you take me for? Of course, I have lube." He kissed me again before rolling to the side and pulling out what we needed from his bedside table.

And then he was over me again, both of us working on each other, not speaking. We didn't need to. I just kissed him, wanting more, *needing* more but knowing that it might be too much if I asked for it. Especially if I begged.

I lay there, his dick in my hand as he worked on me. When he was between my legs, sliding over me, I groaned, the tip of his dick pressing against my entrance.

"You ready?" he asked after he had worked on me enough that I saw stars and was nearly ready to come at a single touch of his cock.

"I've been waiting," I groaned.

Then he pressed inside. Both of us stopped breathing, doing our best not to come. He was big, almost *too* big, but I wanted it. The aching burn was nearly too much. I pumped myself, squeezing my dick as Riggs kept my thighs wide, pressing into me. And then his mouth was on my shoulder, and he was balls-deep. Suddenly, there were no more words. No more thoughts.

He moved, and I arched for him. It was like before, yet it wasn't. We weren't those people anymore, learning each other and fumbling. No, we were men with secrets, pasts. People who couldn't have a future—at least not together.

I groaned, arching up into him again. When I was close to the edge with him rubbing me in just the right place, he reached between us, holding my hand over my dick, and squeezed. And then I came, spilling over my stomach as Riggs groaned, filling the condom.

He kissed me again slowly as we both came down, and I looked up at him. Peered into the face that had filled thousands of vivid dreams for me for as long as I'd known him.

And I knew if I said anything, it would likely be the wrong thing. So, I just kissed him and pretended that I would be okay when I had to walk away.

That I wouldn't think about him again. That I wouldn't regret that this could only be one night.

It had to be.

He was Riggs, and I was Clay.

He was the jock. I was the nerd. He had a life, and my life was my family. I didn't even have time for myself.

Therefore, I didn't have time for Riggs.

Only maybe, just *maybe*, I'd have time for dreams.

If I let myself.

Chapter 3

Clay

I liked working with my hands. I was damn good at it. However, today, it was more work of the mind than anything.

I was the assistant project manager for Montgomery Builders. Meaning, I worked directly under Beckett Montgomery. He was the eldest of five siblings, and each of those Montgomerys worked together at our construction company. I didn't know the entire history of Montgomery Builders or exactly how they came about. However, I did know that Beckett's parents had built the place from the ground up.

Beckett's mother's family, the other Montgomerys, had a construction company of their own called Montgomery Inc. That business was even bigger than the one I currently worked at. They did projects all over Colorado, while Montgomery Builders was a little smaller and tended to focus on two or three projects at a time. Montgomery Inc. was growing by leaps and bounds, while Montgomery Builders was doing the same in their own right.

The elder Montgomery, Beckett's father, used to have a feud with the other Montgomerys down south, though I wasn't sure the other Montgomerys were aware of it.

All I knew was that every time I walked into a business meeting—or what was *supposed* to be a business meeting—when Beckett's father was there, things got weird. The older man used to get egotistical, standoffish, and would insert himself into every part of the project, ignoring his talented children's request to retire like he'd said he would do.

Everything had come to a head over a year earlier. Now, things were finally settling.

The five Montgomery siblings, my bosses, worked well together and were each building families and foundations of their own.

Beckett was marrying Eliza, and the two were in the process of looking into adoption. They were strong together, and Eliza was one of the most beautiful women I had ever seen in my life.

Beckett was a little loud, a bit brash, and would literally take a bullet to save you. Because that's the kind of man he was.

Benjamin, Beckett's twin, was the landscape architect. He had his own team and was rarely in the office. These days, he was with his fiancée, working on and building incredible landscapes in people's yards or for the larger buildings the company worked on.

We didn't just build model homes. We created custom housing and businesses. We were damn good at what we did, and Benjamin made it sing.

But we couldn't do it all without Annabelle. Annabelle Montgomery-Queen was our lead architect and newly married. She joked that she would knock off the name Montgomery and stick with only Queen, but the Montgomery women didn't tend to change their names—or they hyphenated.

To be a Montgomery was to be family. To be truth. All of them had a Montgomery iris, the family's logo and crest tattooed on their bodies. People who married into the family got it, as well.

Paige, the youngest Montgomery and the company's office manager—AKA the person that kept everything running smoothly like a well-oiled machine—had joked that since I had been working with the Montgomerys in one way or another for nearly a decade now, I should get a tattoo of my own.

I had shaken my head, though the idea of having a tight-knit family like that, one that held you when you fell and didn't back down when things got hard, meant a lot.

My connections to the Montgomerys came from the Denver branch and how my life had changed when I was a little kid—when I lost everything, and Storm got hurt in the process.

I'd grown up knowing that Storm would always be there. And when he married Everly, she'd thought of me as family, as well.

I wasn't a kid anymore. And I wasn't a Montgomery.

"Why do you look so sad?" Archer, the final Montgomery and Annabelle's twin asked as he walked in, looking as if he'd just gotten out of a shower. Archer was the lead plumber for Montgomery Builders.

I raised a brow. "I'm fine. Why do you look like you're wet?"

"Because I *am* wet." He winked and grinned. "Should I not say that with an employee?"

"Probably not. But I'm the one who brought it up." Archer pressed his lips together at the word *up*, his eyes dancing. I threw back my head and laughed. "Considering you're a plumber, how many innuendos do you make a day?"

"Thousands, all to myself. I'm not about to make them to my staff." He paused. "And now I could say something about staff, but I won't. However, I did just hit the shower because there was an incident. I don't want to talk about it, but I'm clean now. After three showers, thanks to the lovely full bathroom in my office."

"I guess it helps that you are the plumber and can make sure you get what you need in terms of showers for your office."

"I designed that baby knowing I would use it on certain days when I don't have enough time to go home."

"Well, for all our sakes, I'm glad you're clean."

"Do I want to know?" Beckett asked as he walked in, shaking his head. "No. I don't want to go down that path. Not again." He shuddered. "Never again. Come on, let's get into the main conference room."

I frowned. "I thought we were meeting in your office." The Montgomerys had this strange system where they rotated where they had the main meetings with the group. They alternated offices, making it so nothing got stale, and everybody had an opportunity to feel as if they were comfortable in their place.

"There's a bird outside the window and it won't shut up. I can't think. I don't want to move it because I think it has a nest there, but it's so loud that I might spoon my eyes out. So, no, we're not meeting in my office."

I frowned. "A bird?" I tried not to laugh. Beckett was my boss, after all.

"A bird. I don't want to talk about it." He huffed away, heading towards the conference room, and Archer and I gave each other looks.

"I won't laugh. That means you can't laugh," Archer muttered, the light in his eyes dancing.

"It's going to be hard." Too late, I realized that I'd said the word *hard* to Archer.

"Stop making it so easy for jokes that can get me into trouble." Archer made a strangled sound, and I laughed with him, following him to the meeting room.

"Do I want to know why you're wet?" Paige asked as she shook her head. "No, you're a plumber. There are things that I don't want to know. Ever. Please don't tell me."

"Hey, I'm the one who helped fix the clog in your sink yesterday. For free."

"And I organized your tax stuff for the accountant. I don't know why you're bringing that up," Paige replied, fluttering her eyelashes.

"You do that?" I asked, leaning forward. "The organizing thing."

Paige narrowed her eyes. "Not always, but I owed Archer. Do you need help?"

I cringed. "A little. Things are getting a little more complicated with the bonus you all gave me. Not that I'm complaining."

Paige smiled, her eyes lighting up. "I'll help, but you *do* need an accountant. We have a guy. He does personal taxes, too, not just business."

"How much is that going to cost?" I asked with a wince.

"You'll get the Montgomery discount. You just need to get the tattoo," Annabelle teased as she waddled in.

I would not say the word *waddle* out loud, though, because she would hurt me. And she was really strong for a woman pregnant with twins.

"Okay, let's get this party started," Annabelle stated as she put her feet up.

"Before we do, we're going to ask one thing that is off the record and not on work time. So, nobody's getting paid right now," Benjamin said as he leaned forward. "My wife has a question."

"Oh, yes. I have questions, too." Annabelle winced. "Only we're at work, so I probably shouldn't ask."

I looked between them and swallowed hard. "Is this about the bar?" I asked, not bothering to hide.

Paige blinked. "What bar? Riggs'? What happened at Riggs'?" Her eyes widened. "Oh, *with* Riggs. I have questions. So many questions. I would say we should meet at the bar after work to talk, but maybe we shouldn't."

She rubbed her hands together with glee, and I rolled my eyes. "It's not any of your business," I answered casually, looking between them all.

"It's not, but we're your friends. So, if you'd like to tell us why the two of you left together and were trying to be subtle about it, I would love to know," Archer urged.

I stared at my friend. "You weren't even there."

"I hear things."

I laughed and leaned back in my chair. "Riggs and I have known each other for a long time."

"What?" Beckett asked, his eyes widening. "Really?"

"Really. It's not a big deal. Anyway, we know each other, and that's all I'm going to say."

"Like, know-know, or like *want* to know-know?" Paige asked, holding up her hands. "I get it, break's over. But wow. He's hot."

Thankfully, we started talking about the project, and I leaned back, took notes, and asked questions when I needed to.

Unlike most of the other teams, I was one of the only people who wasn't a Montgomery in these meetings. Most of the other staff was either already on projects or didn't need to be here. They got what they needed directly from their superiors.

Beckett liked me being at the meetings because I asked decent questions, and he wanted me to learn how to do his job. Not that I would ever *have* his job at Montgomery Builders. If I wanted Beckett's role, Montgomery Builders would have to expand—and they might. Or I'd have to find another assignment. I could always go down and work for Montgomery Inc. And thanks to the fact that the feud was no longer in evidence, nobody would hold it against me.

However, I wasn't sure what I wanted yet. Right now, I just wanted to learn. Plus, moving the kids again would be a little too much. They already had enough on their plates.

We finished the meeting and then headed out to the project site. Beckett and I went our separate ways since he didn't have to watch over me every second of every day. Today, while Beckett inspected a few things on Site B, I would get my hands dirty at Site A. I liked the idea of that.

But I couldn't stop thinking about Riggs. And I needed to.

Even as I made sure the Montgomerys didn't ask too many questions and lied to myself, telling myself that it would only be the one time, I knew I didn't want it to be.

Riggs had already texted me this morning, saying that he'd had a good time the weekend before. I hadn't been to the bar since, and hadn't seen him elsewhere either, but that wasn't unusual. There was homework and getting the kids to bed.

I had told him the truth—that I didn't have time. Only I wanted to find a way to *make* time. And that worried me.

By the end of my shift, I was exhausted and grateful that the Montgomerys understood the idea of working parents. I had a lot of paperwork and things I could do at home for work on the clock later. I could take a break to pick up the kids from after-school care or sporting things and move around my hours to make it work. I wished I could afford a nanny, or at least someone to help out. And while I had friends who could give me a hand when needed, we all had lives, and it wasn't easy.

After I finished work at the site, I headed towards Mariah's after-school care. My littlest cousin was five years old and a fricking joy. She was inquisitive, bright, smiley, and today, she had wanted to dress up like an alien princess for school.

Mariah's school was amazing and let the kids dress however they wanted as long as it wasn't their underwear or something that had curse words stitched on it. When I arrived to pick up Mariah, she ran towards me in her princess outfit and alien antennae, her glittered cheeks sparkling, her smile so bright it lit up my world. I hadn't been the one to add the glitter, but from the look of her hands, she might have done it herself during after-school care.

"Clay!" Mariah shouted as she jumped into my arms. I held her close and kissed the top of her head, careful of the headband.

One of the parents gave me an odd look, and I just shifted Mariah on my hip and carried her out to the car. She called me by my first name. She wasn't my daughter, though I had raised her for the past two years.

I would most likely never be Dad to her.

Her dad was Everly's late husband. In our complicated worlds, Mariah's brothers had only known their dad for stolen weekends with my aunt, while my littlest cousin had never known the man at all. When my aunt died after doing some pretty terrible things, I'd slowly ended up in this position.

As a pseudo-father to three kids.

I buckled Mariah in as she talked nonstop about her day, then made my way to pick up Holden and Jackson.

Jackson was eleven and a little know-it-all who wanted to be the man of the house, even though he was kind at the same time.

Holden was quiet, loved animals, and could make me smile and laugh endlessly.

I loved these kids as if they were mine. And, damn it, they *were*. Even if I had no idea what the fuck I was doing most days.

I was twenty-six years old and a father of three.

A *single* father of three at that.

I wasn't supposed to be doing this on my own. And that made me think of Riggs, and what the hell? I'd had one night with him. One night where we'd been adults and living these new lives of ours. That didn't mean there would be anything else.

I pulled into the pickup line right as the boys' school let out and thought I was one of the later parents arriving. I didn't care. The kids would get to me when they got to me, and then I would get home. I still had some work to do but was able to do it from my computer. I also made up hours on weekends. That was when the kids had full babysitting time. I could make up my hours for a full work week on Saturdays, and the Montgomerys were fine with that. We worked when we could. Somehow, I'd lucked out with the best fucking family there was. Montgomery Builders was also working on an in-house daycare with all the upcoming new births—not just in the Montgomery family but also within the staff. It would mimic the one at Montgomery Inc. I thought it was brilliant.

"I can't believe that Jeremiah said that," Jackson mumbled as he got into the car, Holden behind him. Holden was a little pale and quiet and leaned against the back of the seat.

"You okay, buddy?" I asked, looking in the rearview mirror even as I waited for the kids to buckle up.

"We're fine," Jackson said, raising his chin.

"What did Jeremiah do? And don't answer for Holden, Jackson, if I'm asking if he's okay."

Jackson winced. "Sorry. Jeremiah threw up all over Sunshine."

"Sunshine?" I asked.

"That's what she wants to be called today. Yesterday, it was Bunny. Tomorrow, it's probably going to be Rainbow."

I snorted, knowing that the little girl's name was Sarah, but she liked going by different names daily depending on what her imaginary friend wanted. From what I could tell, at least, her teachers didn't mind, and I was grateful that she didn't seem to be getting bullied for it.

Jackson continued. "Anyway, Jeremiah threw up all over her, and she cried, but she didn't hit him like another kid said she should. She just went to change, and Jeremiah went home."

"I take it there's a bug going around then?" I asked, knowing if it hit my house, that was another week off work because it would hit all three kids hard.

"You okay, Holden?" I asked again softly, a bit worried.

Holden nodded, but I felt like that was a lie. The kid had asthma and had to be very careful if he got sick. So, when we got home, I got them snacks as they started on their homework and reached out to press my hand against Holden's forehead.

"I'm fine," he mumbled as he leaned against me, his eyes closed.

"You're hot, buddy. Come on, let's take your temperature."

I cursed under my breath. Noting the temp of one hundred and one, I almost called Everly to ask what I should do next, but I had done this before. I could do it this time, as well. So, I gave him medicine to take the fever down and tucked him into bed. He said his stomach didn't hurt, but he definitely had a bug of some sort.

"Is Holden sick?" Mariah asked, her eyes watery.

I washed my hands and held her close. "I don't know yet, Bug. Let's figure it out."

"I don't want to get sick. We get to play in the clover tomorrow."

I nodded and kissed the top of her head. "Recess?"

"The special recess at the park."

I vaguely remembered that being on the itinerary and nodded again, worried about Holden. I set Mariah down and gave Jackson a look. "I'll be right back. I'm just going to check on him."

"He didn't get to play at recess," Jackson put in, and I froze.

"What?"

"Holden said that he didn't play at recess. That he just sat there because he wasn't feeling good."

I sighed, worried. "Thanks for letting me know."

"I'm sorry I didn't tell you earlier."

I shook my head. "You're telling me now. Thanks for watching out for your brother. I'm going to check on him. Watch your sister, okay? And work on your homework."

"I've got Mariah," Jackson said, raising his chin.

I nodded tightly, knowing that Jackson wanted to control as much as possible because he hadn't had much control in anything before this.

Jackson had been nine when his life was rocked, everything changing.

Nine when he'd come to live with me. He remembered how things were and knew that things weren't ever going back to how they used to be.

I moved towards Holden's bedroom and nearly tripped over myself as I saw him sitting up, clutching his chest.

I ran to him and rubbed his back. "Can you breathe?"

Holden nodded slightly, and I cursed under my breath and reached for his inhaler. We did the steps, and I rubbed his back again, not liking the sound of his breathing.

"I think we need to go to the doctor," I said.

Holden wiped away tears, rubbing his eyes. "I don't want to."

"It's okay, buddy."

"I don't want to be sick."

"Everybody gets sick. Remember when I had a cold? Everybody called me a big baby." I had been, mostly because I'd had to miss work, but mentioning it made Holden smile.

I looked down at my phone, holding back a frown. I wondered if I should call someone for the kids, then remembered that Storm and Everly were just getting back to Denver today from a trip over an hour away.

Most of the other Montgomerys were all still at work, and I didn't want to have a sick kid near any of the pregnant women in my life. Archer was heading out of town to be with his fiancé today, as well.

I was running out of people to call to watch the kids, but I shook my head. It was fine. I would just take them all with me. We'd get their homework, and we'd make do. I had done it before, and I would do it now.

I packed everybody up, careful to watch Holden the entire time. As soon as I got into my SUV, I pressed the button to start the engine, and…nothing happened. My hand shook, and I tried again, pressing the gas, doing anything I could think of, but nothing worked. The screen in front of me blinked a few times, and then the car went silent.

The fucking battery.

It had happened in my last SUV like this, but I hadn't thought it would happen again with this one—not this soon after getting the vehicle.

"What's wrong, Clay?" Mariah asked, her eyes wide, her teeth worrying her lip.

I had positioned her car seat in the very back of the SUV next to Jackson. I wasn't sure what to do. I pulled up my phone, knowing I wasn't going to call a rideshare. I needed to find a friend. Someone to take us to the hospital so I could help my kid.

One name popped up on the screen as I scrolled, and swallowed hard.

Damn it.

Well, I had to hope that he wouldn't mind. Because I didn't know who else to call, and if I kept thinking, it would take more time, and I would panic.

I pressed the button and hoped like hell that Riggs answered.

Chapter 4

Riggs

"Neil did what now?" Delilah asked as she sat next to me on the couch. Delilah was a friend from high school. We'd known each other for years, though she had been a goth cheerleader who hadn't quite fit in, and I had been the bisexual jock who'd hidden my sexuality from most people until college.

Clay had been the quiet kid, the brilliant one. The one I had crushed on hard when no one was looking. Back then, even though people were coming out in high school—those who had a better sense of self than I had—most kids still hid who they were from their families and from themselves.

Clay and I finding each other for those brief moments spoke volumes. The fact that nobody had even known what had happened between the two of us, including Delilah at the time, was a miracle.

I had never wanted to put Clay in a position where he might regret what had happened. Including last weekend. However, we weren't talking about Clay. No, Delilah and I were talking about my actual bad decision, not the questionable one.

"He showed up at the bar."

"Don't tell me he wants you back," Delilah grumbled, taking a sip of her martini.

Delilah owned a prominent lesbian club in Denver. I even helped behind the bar every once in a while—just like she did for me at Riggs' when I needed it. We were each other's way to take a vacation, though taking one together was nearly unheard of.

I had to go in tonight and work, and Delilah was coming with me. She wouldn't have to lift a finger unless she wanted. Although, given the way she was at my place, once she was behind the bar, she thrived. She lit up the place nearly every time and ended up going home with a beautiful woman by the end of the evening. That was Delilah. She was just brilliant in that way.

"He doesn't want me back. I'm not going to *take* him back anyway. He was there, and…something was weird about him. I don't know what it was."

"Well, just be careful. Neil is an asshole who always gets what he wants. Thankfully, he didn't get your bar. He didn't get your money. But you know he's fuming about that."

I looked down at my lime and soda and frowned. "I know. It's not like he can actually take Riggs' from me." Alarm shot through me. "Right?"

"Right. He can't. And if he tries, then we'll just castrate him." Delilah smirked.

I rolled my eyes. "Please, don't. Don't even say things like that. Because then I'm an accessory to your deeds."

"Oh, yes, because it's all about keeping your ass out of jail."

"You know it."

She snorted, shaking her head. "Other than your ex acting fucking weird, anything else?"

I shook my head. "Nope. Everything is good."

Delilah blinked. "Okay, tell me what happened. Because…wow, that was such a lie you just said right then. I can taste it." She set down her drink and leaned forward.

When she patted my knee, I narrowed my eyes. "Don't try to hit on me to get answers."

"I would hit on you so well, you wouldn't even know it was happening. And I'm not even into guys."

"Really? You think I'm that easy?" I asked dryly.

"I'm serious. Now, tell me. What happened?"

I might as well lay it all out there since I was bursting at the seams with needing to tell *someone*. "I slept with Clay. Again."

Delilah blinked a few times and then leaned back, her hand over her heart. "I'm glad I wasn't holding my drink just then because, whoa. Really? I'd ask how he was, but we know it was great. You wouldn't be so befuddled if it weren't. And, wow. Are you guys together now? After all this time? Oh my God, I feel like I need to go dance or something. This is amazing. All of my high school dreams and giddiness are coming through. It's like an episode of *Dawson's Creek*. Tell me what's going on with Pacey. Are Pacey and Dawson finally getting together? Oh, no, it's Pacey and Jack, isn't it? We don't like Dawson. Oh, I don't know. This is so exciting." She started clapping her hands together and bounced.

I did my best not to laugh. *"Dawson's Creek* is the show you went with, not anything more recent?"

"It was the only thing that came to mind. That or *Buffy the Vampire Slayer*. So are we going with the Spike and Angel thing? Not Xander. Neil can be Xander."

I laughed outright, knowing her hatred of Xander knew no bounds. Frankly, I was the same way, but I wasn't going to give her the satisfaction of saying that.

"Now that you're through thinking of late '90s and early 2000s shows from the WB or CW—whatever it's called now—know that Clay is a friend. I think. Anyway, it's just casual. Just the one time. He's swamped. He has three kids."

Delilah's eyes filled with emotion as she nodded, biting her lip. "I remember hearing about all of that, considering most of it happened down in Denver."

"It was horrible, but he's doing an excellent job with those kids. The fact that he even had a night off to spend with me is a big thing."

"Then it's just casual, and it's never going to happen again?"

I shrugged, trying not to care too much about what I was feeling. And totally failing. "It is casual. I'll see him again when he comes into the bar, but that's about it. He rarely comes in. He can't do more. He needs help, and I don't know how to do that other than to just be there when he has time." I frowned and looked down at my lime and soda again. "I don't know how I feel about that, but I don't know what else to do, either."

Delilah reached out and squeezed my hand. "It's okay. You're allowed to feel sad that it might not be the right time. Clay was a great kid back when I remember him. And whenever you talk about him, at least when you did before this, you always got that smile on your face. So, yay. You finally slept with Clay again. I just hope you're not too sad that you may not be able to have a repeat performance."

"There's plenty of fish in the sea. As long as they aren't named Neil, I'm fine."

She smiled then, and my phone buzzed. I looked down at it, blinking.

"Who is it?" she asked, leaning back on the couch. "What's got that look on your face?"

"Speak of the devil."

"Neil?"

"No, the good devil," I corrected, letting out a hollow laugh before answering. "Hey there, Clay. What's up?"

"I know this is awkward timing and out of the blue, but do you think you can come and help me take the kids to the emergency room?"

I stood before he'd even finished the sentence. "Give me your address, and I'm right there."

"I'm sorry about this."

"It's fine. I've got you. Do you need to call an ambulance?"

Delilah stood next to me, her drink long forgotten, her eyes wide at my words.

"No, we just need to get to the ER so I can get Holden some meds. It's happened before, and my fucking car won't start."

I heard the rumble in his voice as my heart raced. I ran to the front door and slid my feet into my shoes. "Text me the address. I'll be there as soon as I can. If you need anything else, just let me know. I'll be right there."

"Thanks, Riggs. I just...thanks."

He hung up, and my phone buzzed with the address.

"It doesn't sound casual," Delilah stated and then shook herself. "Sorry. That's not what I meant. Is everything okay? Is it the kids?"

"He says one of them needs meds and has to go to the ER. And his car won't start. I don't know, but I'm freaking the fuck out. I've got to go."

"Of course. Go save the day. Protect those kids. Protect your heart. And maybe just let someone love you."

I looked at her and snorted before leaning in and smacking a hard kiss on her lips. "You're losing your damn mind." I closed my eyes. "Fuck. The bar." I'd completely forgotten my bar, my reason for getting up in the morning, with a single phone call.

Delilah waved me off. "I had two sips of my drink. I've got this. I've got the keys, and I can close. I can do whatever you need. Get those kids their meds or whatever the hell they need and help Clay. He called you, Riggs. He called *you*."

I swallowed hard. "Yeah, he did."

I left her place at my place, knowing that she would take care of the bar, even as I had to somehow figure out what the hell I was doing.

Clay only lived about five minutes from my house, surprisingly. How I had never seen him in the neighborhood before was beyond me, but I pulled into a small ranch-style home with blue shutters and a roof that probably needed to be redone. Considering that he worked for a construction company and was a builder himself, Clay probably knew that, but money didn't grow on trees—even with the Montgomery discount.

I pulled in behind a large SUV and hoped to hell that everyone would be able to fit in mine.

"Thank you," Clay said as he came walking forward, a kid hanging over his shoulder, wheezing slightly. Clay had a large car seat in one hand and a manic expression on his face.

An older kid followed with a booster in his hand. And a little girl with a bright pink bag trailed behind, her eyes wide.

I'd never met Clay's cousins before, and this hadn't been how I imagined it happening.

"I didn't even ask if you could fit everybody in your car." Clay shook his head, the panic wafting off of him.

"It's okay. I've got this." I moved forward and took the car seat from Clay and the booster from the oldest kid. "Okay, let's do this quickly so I can figure out how to fit everybody in. We can make it work."

My SUV had three rows just like Clay's car, and I was glad that I had bought the larger one for moving things around for the bar versus the little sports car I'd thought I would get after my divorce.

The oldest kid helped me figure out how to set everything up as the littlest one jumped into the car seat and buckled herself in. Clay set up Holden, the middle child, in the booster seat.

"I'm Mariah. Holden's sick," the little girl chirped with wide eyes.

I swallowed hard and looked at her little pigtails. "It looks like it. We're going to get him all fixed up."

"It's okay. He has asthma."

She said it with such aplomb that I nodded. "Good to know."

The oldest kid moved forward. "That's Holden. I'm Jackson. Thank you for driving us."

Jackson moved to the back row, his gaze narrowed on me before he focused on watching over his siblings.

I pulled on Clay's shoulder as he kept trying to tuck in Holden even more and wrap a blanket around him.

"Come on, get in the car. I'll get us to the emergency room."

"St. Mary's," he whispered and shook his head. "That's the emergency room we go to. His pediatrician is closed now, or I would just take him there."

"I've got this. Get in the passenger seat. I have one of those little mirror things that pops down so you can check on the kids so you're not craning your neck. *We've* got this."

Clay looked around, picked up a bag I hadn't seen, and shoved it into the back seat with Jackson before hopping into the passenger seat.

"We've got this," Clay whispered, repeating my words. "Thank you."

I pulled out onto the road and went the exact speed limit. I'd never really driven with kids in the car before, and I had no idea what I was doing.

"Turn right up here," Clay said.

My lips crept into a smile. "I'm friends with the Montgomerys, too. I know where the hospital is."

Clay winced and nodded. There was a running joke with the Montgomerys that in each city they lived in, they tried to have a wing of their own at the hospital. Considering how many incidents happened within that family, it was a little worrying to be friends with them. You never knew when you'd end up back in that waiting room.

We pulled into the emergency room lot, and Clay pointed off to the side. "Just park, and we'll carry them in. That way, we're all together and don't leave you behind."

I nodded, sweat breaking out. I hadn't thought of the logistics of what was about to happen. "Okay, you got me all night."

Clay blinked. "I mean…I guess. Crap. I'm sorry. Don't you have to work?"

I met Clay's gaze and knew we didn't have a lot of time. And I didn't want to touch him in front of his kids, just in case they didn't know anything about Clay's personal life. Plus, I didn't know what Clay wanted. It was so not the time, and my brain wasn't working right. "I've got it. You've got me for the night."

"Thank you." Relief flooded his features before he moved quickly.

Jackson was already getting out of the car as I moved around and took the bags from him.

"Okay, I've got a pink unicorn bag and this gray one that might be Clay's?"

"I've got Clay's bag," Jackson ordered softly. "You get Mariah's."

"I'm tired," Mariah said with a yawn as she unbuckled herself from her car seat and held out her hands. "And hungry."

I swallowed hard and then plucked her out of the car, settling her on my hip. When was the last time I'd held a child? I didn't know. She had to be what, five? Wasn't that what Clay had said once?

What the hell was I doing?

Clay looked at all of us, Mariah in my arms, and blinked before giving me a tight nod. "Okay, in we go."

We walked into the emergency room, and I was grateful to see that it wasn't too busy. Jackson clung to Clay's side as he and Holden made their way through, and I kept Mariah in my arms.

"I've got to go check in. Jackson? Go sit with Riggs and Mariah, okay?"

"I want to go with you," Jackson whispered.

"I need to make sure Holden is all set up. Can you make sure that Riggs knows what he's doing with Mariah? It's a little daunting with the three of you. I'm just saying." Clay winked as he said it, a smile playing on his face, and I knew that was exactly the right thing to say. Give Jackson a job, and the oldest kid seemed to understand. He came to my side and raised his chin. "Let's go sit down. I can take care of Mariah."

My lips crept into a smile, even though there wasn't much to smile about with Holden being so sick.

"I appreciate the confidence and the help." I met Clay's gaze. "Go. I've got them."

Clay looked like he wanted to say something, but there wasn't any time. The nurse took one look at Holden, and they brought Clay and Holden to the back. The fact that they did it so quickly, even as Clay filled out the paperwork, worried me, but I tried not to let it show. Instead, I set Mariah down on one of the chairs, took a seat next to her, and looked over at Jackson, who sat next to the little girl.

Mariah held her bag close, then pulled out her little pink tablet and earbuds.

"Only twenty minutes. It's a weeknight," Jackson whispered.

"I'll be okay."

"What's only twenty minutes?" I asked.

"Her show. It's a weeknight, and we're not allowed to watch a lot of TV because we have school and then bed."

I nodded. "Good to know because I don't know what I'm doing. I'm just here to make sure that you guys are safe."

Jackson narrowed his eyes at me. "I thought one of the Montgomerys would come. Clay said they were all busy or out of town."

I swallowed hard, wondering what the hell I should be saying. "Well, you've got me. Don't worry, we'll just stay right here and make sure that we're here when Clay comes out."

"I have to go to the bathroom," Mariah said suddenly, taking out her earbuds, even though she had just put them in.

Alarm shot through me. Fear, panic, and everything that could connect to that emotion.

Germs surrounded us, but there was a small family restroom across the way. What was I supposed to do? Leave Jackson with the chairs? Did I let Mariah go by herself? That didn't seem right.

Jackson sighed and stuffed everything back into Mariah's bag. "Come on. I've got you."

I cleared my throat, oddly relieved Jackson knew what he was doing. "I'll go with you."

"You can't go into the bathroom with her," Jackson whined as if he were a forty-year-old matron.

"No, but we can stand outside the door." I paused. "You are potty-trained, right?" I asked Mariah.

Mariah giggled. "Of course, I am. I'm not a baby."

"I don't know these things. You guys have to teach me."

Mariah skipped her way to the bathroom, something I would never be able to do, let alone if I had to pee, but I didn't try to think about it. She went into the restroom and closed the door by herself as Jackson spoke through the other side of the door. "Don't lock it."

"What if someone comes in?" Mariah asked.

"We're here. We won't let anyone go in," Jackson countered.

I nodded. "Sounds like a plan." I didn't relish figuring out how to break a kid out of a bathroom if Mariah locked herself inside. I looked at Jackson as he folded his arms in front of him.

"Holden will be okay," I said, hoping to hell I wasn't lying.

He scrunched up his face. "He has asthma. Anytime it gets a little cold, it turns into something more. I hate it."

I swallowed hard. "I'm sorry. That's got to be scary."

"I'm not scared. I just said I hate it."

I nodded. "Okay, then."

"I just wish Storm and Everly were here. They could help. That way, Clay wouldn't have to call you."

I blinked. "I'm sorry I'm here then."

"I don't know you. Holden's going to be scared, and Mariah will be, too. They need someone they know."

Not sure where I stood with the kid, I nodded. "Clay knows me. So, let's get to know each other."

Jackson narrowed his eyes at me before nodding tightly. "Okay."

The sound of water running and a little girl giggling filled my ears, and then the door opened, and Mariah threw paper towels into the trash receptacle before walking out. "All done. And I washed my hands. And I used the paper towel on the door handle like Clay taught us."

My lips threatened to quirk into a smile, but I nodded solemnly. "Very germ conscientious."

"I don't like germs," Mariah said, shaking her head.

"Me, either. Let's go get our seats back since they're still open."

"Okay," Mariah said as she skipped her way to her seat.

Jackson and I followed, and we got back into position, waiting to hear anything from Clay.

I had my phone out, anticipating a text. When it buzzed, I looked down at the screen and held back a curse—no need to scare the kids.

Instead, I hit ignore on Neil's name and told myself I should just block his number.

Jackson gave me a weird look, and I shrugged, not bothering to explain to a kid I didn't even know why I was ignoring my ex-husband.

We had enough on our plates. I didn't need to add the drama that was my life to the drama that seemed to be Clay's.

Only Clay had called me.

He had asked for help, and I'd dropped everything for him.

I had no idea what I was supposed to do with that.

Chapter 5

Clay

I would not fall asleep. I would not fall asleep.

I kept up that mantra as I watched Holden breathe, looking so tiny in the big hospital bed, the nebulizer keeping him steady. He was down for the count for the evening and would have to stay overnight as soon as there was a bed for him upstairs. They were admitting him for twenty-four hours to keep watch because they were afraid that he would end up getting pneumonia even after less than a day of this cold. Because that was Holden. He never did anything the easy way.

My lips threatened to smile, even if there was nothing funny about any of this. Holden was so thoughtful, so purposeful, but he also never did anything small. Jackson was pushier, more aggressive in protecting his family, even though he had a kind heart. And Mariah was all kindness and rainbows and puppies but vicious if anyone came at her family.

My kids were fantastic, and I was so scared that I was doing everything wrong.

I hadn't signed up for this. I hadn't signed up for any of it.

I had been a child when my aunt showed up pregnant the first time. Rachel hadn't told anyone who the father was, other than it was a gentleman who loved her.

Then she had gotten pregnant again, and then again. Mariah was actually the same age as Everly's twins. Everly's bastard of a husband had gotten both Rachel *and* Everly pregnant at nearly the same time, and had ended up with five children.

Five kids who had never known their siblings existed until the bastard died in a commuter plane crash. Everly had been pregnant with the twins at the time and had gone into labor because of the stress. Rachel had had Mariah only a few days earlier.

The asshole hadn't met any of them.

I didn't want to hate the man because hate in my heart wasn't good for the soul, but it was hard not to. Rachel had made many poor decisions and then some violent ones that had threatened everything. She had hurt Everly, had hurt my family, and then she had died tragically.

When I ended up with full custody of my cousins, things had changed. I'd had to become a father.

"Mr. Hollings?"

I looked up at the nurse. "Yes? Is there something wrong?"

"Nothing's wrong. I just wanted to check on you and let you know that the man out front with the two children asked how you were doing. We can't let him know anything because he's not on any paperwork, but I figured I'd let you know that there's someone out front."

I nodded and then cursed under my breath. "Sorry. Can you stay here with Holden? He doesn't like to be alone."

The nurse gave me a soft smile. "Of course. If I'm not here, one of the other nurses will be. Someone Holden can trust. He won't be alone. We'll be able to bring him upstairs for the rest of the evening soon."

I nodded and ran my hand through my hair. "Thanks. I need to check on the other kids."

She smiled, and I walked down the winding hallway towards the waiting room. I had already checked on them a few times, scared to leave Holden. Riggs and I had been texting, but my phone was nearly dead, and I hadn't brought my charger. I usually had one in my go-bag for these types of occasions, but I couldn't find it. I kept messing things up. I needed to be better than this.

I walked out into the near-empty waiting room, darkness from the tinted windows spreading across the floor. I nearly tripped over my feet when I saw Riggs there.

He had his phone in his hand, a frown on his face. Mariah slept on his lap with her little coat over her shoulders, and Jackson leaned against Riggs' other shoulder, his mouth open as he snored gently.

I wanted to use the rest of my phone battery to take a photo, but I knew that would be odd. Riggs wasn't their dad. He wasn't even my boyfriend. Yet he had stayed here for hours.

He was watching my kids.

And I trusted him implicitly.

What the hell was I supposed to do? It wasn't supposed to be like this.

Riggs shifted a bit as Jackson moved, but didn't seem to notice me. I leaned forward, and Riggs looked up at me, his eyes wide.

I did what I wanted to do, knowing it could be a mistake, but I didn't care. I just needed this. I pressed a gentle kiss to his lips, barely a brush of pressure, and Riggs smiled softly. "Thank you," I whispered.

Riggs grinned then, his eyes brightening. He was so damn sexy. So damn caring. And he was so much trouble. "Kid okay?"

That was the first thing he asked. A kiss out of nowhere, a long night in a hospital with kids that weren't his, and he was worried about Holden.

Riggs had always been a danger to my heart. A full adult Riggs with a caring soul? Damn near treacherous against my motivations.

"He'll be okay. They're going to keep him overnight."

Riggs sighed. "Okay, then. You going to stay with him?"

"I have to."

"Do you need me to get the kids home? They're passed out here, but they'd probably like to be in their own beds. I don't mind."

I wanted to sit down next to him and hold him close. Just let Riggs tell me that everything would be okay. I didn't want to do everything on my own anymore. I just wanted to breathe and be happy and figure out exactly who I could be as Clay, the man who could maybe fall in love one day. Not Clay, the single father of three with the tragic backstory—far more tragic than anyone else could ever know.

I shook my head after a moment, finally answering Riggs' question. "Storm and Everly are on their way. They cut the trip short and are picking up the kids before they get the twins and their baby."

Riggs blinked. "All the way from Denver?"

"They all have the same routine. They've got this. I did something similar for them when they needed an emergency contact for one of the twins."

Storm and Everly's youngest, Brooklyn, was one now. She wasn't biologically related to my kids, but they all acted as if Brooklyn was their sister as the twins were their siblings. It was the same with the rest of the Denver Montgomerys. Now, it was turning out to be the same with the Fort Collins Montgomerys. They had adopted us, and I figured maybe I should get that tattoo, after all.

Or maybe I just needed sleep.

"I'll stay here until they arrive. I don't mind staying. I'm here for the long haul, Clay."

The way he said that worried me. Because I didn't think it was just for the night. And I didn't know if I was ready for that. Before I could think of anything to say, to thank him again or say I needed to go, Storm and Everly walked in. They looked exhausted, but then again, so was I.

"You're out here. Good. We don't have to go rush and find you," Everly said as I stood up. She threw her arms around me. "Everyone okay?" she asked, her voice low.

I kissed Everly on the top of her head and squeezed her hard. "We're fine."

"Good. The twins, Brooklyn, and Randy—our puppy," Storm added for Riggs' benefit, "are with Wes and Jillian. We don't have to go back to Denver tonight."

I winced. "I didn't think this whole process through, did I?" I asked, running my hands through my hair.

"It's okay. We're good with the logistics while you worry about Holden." Everly smiled. "You're Riggs, then? Clay said that you helped out. We're so grateful."

Riggs waved over Mariah's head. "No problem. We had a good night of TV shows and sleeping."

"We also ate McDonald's," Jackson whispered, and I realized that he had woken up.

He rubbed his eyes, and I gave Riggs a look. "McDonald's?"

"It was close. We ate in the car because I didn't feel like bringing fast food into an emergency room." Riggs shrugged. "You guys missed dinner, remember? I texted you."

I rubbed my stomach and nodded. "Thanks. I know you said you were going to handle it, but everything happened so quickly back there. I'm just grateful."

"As I said, Clay, I don't mind."

Mariah woke up at that moment, while Everly and Storm had so many questions in their eyes I couldn't even find the answers for them. They kept staring between the two of us before Riggs cleared his throat. "Now that you're up, Mariah monster, why don't you hang out with Miss Everly and Mr. Storm while I make sure Clay's okay?"

"Okay," Mariah said softly as she held out her hands.

Storm smiled and picked up Mariah, holding her close. Everly and Riggs changed seats, and Riggs stood and did a complicated handshake with Jackson, both of them fist-bumping on their way out. Riggs leaned down, kissed Mariah on the top of her head, and then nodded at me.

I hadn't been gone that long, but the three of them had bonded.

Bonded so much that it fucking worried me.

Storm gave me a look, and I gestured towards the front door. "I'm going to walk Riggs out."

"No problem. We have car seats in our car, but you may want to get the booster out," Storm said as he tossed me keys.

I nodded, feeling as if I were two steps behind.

"I'll help you move everything," Riggs said as we walked towards the car.

"I don't know what to say," I whispered after a few moments of awkward silence that didn't feel all that awkward.

We stood outside now by Riggs' car, thankfully only two vehicles down from Storm's. We'd already moved the booster seat, and now I wasn't sure what to do next.

Riggs just shook his head and leaned forward. "I'm here for you. I'm sorry tonight was stressful, but you didn't have to do it alone."

Tears pricked my eyes, and I hated myself for it. When Riggs leaned forward more and brushed his lips against mine, I moaned, just wanting to *be* for the moment. To pretend that everything was normal, and this wasn't another complication.

Riggs brushed his thumb across my stubbled jaw before kissing me again. "This isn't going to be simple, Clay. You know that. I don't mind."

"I took your whole night, Riggs. I'm the dad who isn't a dad. I'm the epitome of complicated."

Riggs just snorted and kissed me again. "And I'm a man who doesn't mind helping. I like you, Clay. Remember that."

He kissed me again, and I hated myself. Because I wanted this. I wanted this to be something more. I had relied on him, and he had stepped up to the plate.

And I had no idea what that meant.

"I'll see you tomorrow."

I shook my head, my mind spinning. "I'm not coming into the bar, Riggs. I can't even go into work."

"My friend from out of town is watching the bar. I've got you. I'll see you tomorrow." He kissed me again, and then he walked to the driver's side door, leaving me behind. I watched him go, more confused than ever. This wasn't what I had planned, and yet nothing I did seemed to be working out well.

I locked Storm's car after making sure the booster was in correctly before heading back to the waiting room, surprised to only see Storm there with the kids.

"Everly's on your emergency contact list, so she went back to be with Holden. I will go get the kids set up at your house now that you're back. We wanted to give you a minute to say goodbye to Riggs, or we would've gone out there with you."

I nodded, feeling confused.

"Is Everly staying tonight, then?"

Storm just smiled. "Of course, she is. We tossed a coin to see who would stay with you and the kids, and we both won."

My lips twitched, and I shook my head at the man who was like an older brother, a father, and a friend all rolled into one. "Thank you. Seriously."

"Of course. We're family." He cleared his throat. "Hey, Mariah, go help Jackson finish packing up your bag. Give me a minute to talk to Clay?"

"Okay," Mariah said as Jackson gave us looks but went to pack up her little bag anyway.

"Seriously, thanks for coming tonight. I know it's a long drive."

"We've done it before. So have you. It's what we do. Those kids have you, Clay. Who do you have?"

I blinked at the suddenness of his question, and I shook my head. "I can't think about that right now. I have to go back to Holden."

"Of course, you do. And, of course, you can't think. Maybe you should try, though."

I looked at Storm but I didn't say anything. I didn't have answers. Instead, I said goodbye to the kids and Storm and headed back to the room. Everly smiled softly as she read a book to Holden, who was now awake, his eyes drowsy.

She didn't say anything, even though I knew she had questions, as well.

I sat down next to Everly and watched my kid, wondering what I was thinking.

This was my lot. This was my family.

I wasn't going to get the happily ever after that Storm and Everly had. That Abigail, Archer, Beckett, and Benjamin all had.

This was my path. I didn't get to have Riggs.

I just had to make myself believe that because wishing only hurt.

And promises were meant to be broken when the only promise you had left was to protect your kids—and not yourself.

Chapter 6

Riggs

The bar was packed tonight, a bachelor party raging in the corner. Two of them were regulars but the bachelor wasn't. Everybody was polite even while drinking heavily, but there were three designated drivers, and people were just enjoying themselves. So far. I wasn't going to say that out loud for fear of jinxing it, but there was no fighting, only a good time to be had.

I didn't mind bachelor and bachelorette parties as long as they didn't destroy my bar or annoy others in the process.

These were just guys who seemed to be enjoying themselves. They laughed a little loudly but controlled themselves otherwise.

While we were working on that corner, we also focused on the rest of the packed bar. Some people were dancing. Others watched the game. I had my hair tied back tonight, the stub of a ponytail not the most flattering thing, but I was tired of hair getting in my eyes, and I was working the bar as quickly as I could.

I had to close tonight and then had some paperwork to do back in the office before I headed home.

By taking a couple of days off earlier in the week to hang out with Delilah and then help Clay, I'd gotten a little bit behind. Nothing to be worried about, but my job seemed unending. While I loved it, it was a lot to deal with sometimes.

I pulled a couple of more drafts, and then frowned when one came up empty.

"I need to go change the keg," I called out. Rosie nodded, picking up my slack. I went to the back, grunted as I had to move things around, and did what I did best. I worked.

All I could do was focus on work and not on what I wanted to do.

I wanted to call Clay and see how he was doing. I wanted to check on Holden to see if he was feeling any better. And I wanted to check on Jackson and Mariah because those kids had captured my heart, and I kind of hated it.

I liked them. Jackson was all territorial and grumpy until you got to know him and realized that he just wanted to take care of his family. Mariah was bright and sunny and very particular but would give anything just to be near her brothers.

I shook my head, pushing away thoughts of the family that wasn't mine. But they were tangled around my heart. By the time I finished setting up everything and headed back out, I was tired and a little grumpy.

The problem was, I wanted what I couldn't have.

Just because we had kissed again in the parking lot, and just because Clay seemed to have wanted it as much as I did, didn't mean it would happen. He had his whole life in front of him, and it was filled with bake sales, soccer games, and sick kids. He didn't have time for a guy who worked too many hours at a bar with a past he would rather not think about.

I shook my head, ignoring the little voice in the back of my mind, and went back to work.

When the man in the suit walked through the doors, the hair on the back of my neck stood on end. I glared at him, wondering what the hell this guy who was clearly out of place in my bar wanted.

He met my gaze, tilted his head, and smirked. Why did that smirk remind me so much of Neil?

"Riggs Kennedy?"

I lifted my chin. "You've got him."

"Good. You've been served." He handed over an envelope, and I blinked, looking down at the papers in my hand.

Only a few other people had noticed, mostly my staff and the sober guys in the bachelor party. They frowned at me, and I realized that one of them was Lee, a friend of the Montgomerys. He walked over to me, and I shook my head. "Go hang out with your friends. I've got this."

Lee tilted his head and took the papers from me. "Let me see them. Because I have a feeling you're going to want to Hulk smash something if we're not careful."

"I always thought I was more of a Captain America than a Hulk."

Lee snorted and shook his head. "Come on, do you know what this is about?"

I swallowed hard. "I think I have an idea, and I don't want to get into it here." I gestured to the office area and knew that the rest of my staff could handle everything up front. They would be curious, but I needed a minute.

Lee followed me back, the papers still in his hands. I was glad that he was holding them because I wanted to shred them. Tear them up into tiny pieces so I never had to see them again. Only I didn't think that was legal or would help the situation in the slightest.

I squared my shoulders. "Let me open them."

"You sure you don't want me to?" Lee asked, raising a brow.

"I think that might be illegal."

"True, but if you're watching me do it, is it?" Lee asked as he handed over the folder.

I let out a sigh and opened the envelope. I should've known what I'd see. Neil was always good with scare tactics.

"Well?"

"My ex-husband is suing me for my bar. Citing something about what was owed to him in the divorce. Fucking asshole."

Lee blinked at me. "I didn't even know you were married."

"It was over in a blink, at least it seemed so at the time. But the tendrils of my mistakes do love to seep into my waking hours. Probably until the end of time."

"He doesn't have a leg to stand on, does he?"

I snorted and shook my head, worried. "He shouldn't. Only he has a shit ton of money, better lawyers than I do, and I am exhausted."

Lee reached out and squeezed my shoulder. "Why don't you meet me with the rest of the guys tomorrow."

I frowned, confused. "How the hell is that going to help?"

"Because you're our friend, Riggs. You may think of yourself as being on the periphery like I sometimes do, but the Montgomerys adopted you. And considering you're dating Clay, you're part of us now."

It took me a full minute to catch up to everything he was saying. "How did you know that? And we're not dating. We, well...we're not dating." I didn't want to get into full details of what we had. Lee just rolled his eyes.

"You're dating. No matter if it's a hookup or more. He called you in his time of need. We all know. He could have called me. I was off that day. He could have called anybody, and they would have driven to him. But you were the one that his brain immediately went to when he was in trouble. Clay is one of ours, like a kid brother who's actually older than most of us."

I laughed. "I don't understand you guys."

"I'm not a Montgomery, either, but I've been assimilated into them. It happens. We end up liking it in the end. However, talk it out with us. Talk to your lawyer. But you're going to be there tomorrow. With coffee."

"I have to bring my own coffee for this?" I felt like I was two steps behind, maniacal laughter threatening.

Lee laughed, shaking his head. "I said that wrong. We'll bring the coffee. And danishes. And maybe we'll even have Brenna make us a breakfast cake."

"What's a breakfast cake?" I asked.

"Cake you have for breakfast. Duh."

I laughed, glad that Lee was here. I was stressing out, and I didn't know what I was supposed to do, but Lee made me smile. He was a good guy. We had flirted on occasion when I first opened the bar, but nothing had ever come of it.

Probably because Clay was always in the back of my mind, damn it.

"I don't have a choice, do I?"

"You don't. I mean, you *do* because they're not rudely pushy, but I am. So, get your ass there. And tell us what the hell's going on. I promise we won't annoy you with Clay questions."

I raised a brow. "Really?"

"We won't invite the women. Therefore, they won't gossip."

I blinked, shocked at his words. "That's sexist of you."

Lee just laughed. "And completely a lie because we're way worse when it comes to gossip. Just saying."

I laughed, shook my head, and set the papers on my desk. "I need to work, call my lawyer, and…I guess I'll see you tomorrow."

"You damn well will because we like Riggs'. It's our place to go. So, we're not going to let someone fuck it up. I'm very selfish when it comes to this."

"Good to know," I said with a laugh and shook my head.

I followed Lee out of the office, ignored the look on my staff's faces, and told myself that this was fine and that I could handle it.

Only I was pretty sure that was a lie.

The next morning, I headed over to Jacob Queen's place. He was married to Annabelle Montgomery and was a friend of mine. The place next door had once been Annabelle's, but now they were renting it out to other people. At one point, I knew Eliza had lived there, but she'd moved in with Beckett, and the new renters who'd moved in had gotten orders out of state so it might be empty once again.

I shook my head, confused at the real estate in Colorado. I had a decent-sized home. It wasn't the best, but it did well enough. I was a renter too because I couldn't afford a house and a bar, and if Neil had anything to say about it, I would lose that, too. I held back a small groan and did my best to ignore the feelings threatening to take over my sanity.

I knocked on the door, and Archer answered, a grin on his face. "There you are. Come on in. We've got coffee, danishes, and what Brenna called a breakfast cake."

"A breakfast cake is just a cake you eat for breakfast. There's not sausages or anything in it." Lee groaned. "Why don't you guys understand the concept of breakfast cake?"

"Because it's a dessert cake that you're calling breakfast just so you can eat it in the morning," Beckett said with a grin, coffee in hand. "You're here. Good," he looked at me. "Now we can talk about what the fuck is going on with your bar."

"You told them?" I asked Lee, blinking.

Lee shrugged. "Well, we were already having a morning to discuss upcoming bachelor parties and all of that. And then I said you'd be joining us because of an issue with your bar."

"Oh," I said before looking around and noticing everyone else there.

Archer had taken a seat, his latte in hand. Benjamin sat next to him, an equally highly decorated latte in his grip. Archer's fiancé, Marc, stood next to the window, phone in use, but he gave me a wave before going back to his conversation.

Then there was Clay, sending my senses into overdrive with the sexy just-woke-up look about him. He stood in the kitchen with two mugs of coffee in hand and a small smile on his face. "You've been trapped. Just know that there is no way out. Now that the Montgomerys have officially assimilated you, you'll either get tattooed or be brainwashed. There is no middle ground."

"Why would there be a middle ground between tattooing and

brainwashing?" Archer asked after he'd taken a sip of his drink. "They're clearly on the same path."

"Shut up," Clay said with a roll of his eyes before handing me the extra mug in his hand.

I nodded my thanks. "Hey. Didn't know you'd be here."

Talk about awkward. I felt everybody's eyes on me, but I ignored them and just focused on Clay. Clay gave me a small smile and then took a sip of his drink. "Of course, I'm here. Someone's trying to hurt you. What did you think we'd do?"

"I don't know," I whispered. "I didn't expect this."

"Well, you should. I mean, we do have a lawyer here. And this is his house."

Jacob came in, rubbing the back of his neck. "Yes, I am a lawyer. Do you have one?" he asked, and I nodded.

"I do."

I named the firm, and Jacob nodded tightly. "They're good. They know what they're talking about. If you need someone else, I've got you."

I snorted. "I can't afford your rates, Jacob."

"For my favorite bar? I'd do it pro bono."

"Don't let Annabelle hear you say that because you guys have twins coming. You can't just go off giving free advice to anyone," Archer teased.

Marc ended his phone call and sat next to Archer, undoing his suit coat buttons as he did. Everyone else was in casualwear, but Marc looked like he had just stepped out of the office. I was honestly surprised to see him. He rarely came to the bar anymore as he worked so many hours, but he was engaged to Archer, and the two looked happy.

The only person who wasn't here was Colton, Paige's man. I didn't know the story there, but there had to be a reason he was absent. Not that I would say anything. Sometimes it paid to be silent and listen when you wanted answers.

Except everyone was staring at me. Apparently, I was supposed to speak.

"Tell us what's going on," Jacob urged as he pulled out a pad and paper.

"You're really going to work?" I asked with a laugh, oddly shocked—and touched.

"I like notes. It's a legal pad. I'm a lawyer. That's what I do."

"Just tell us," Clay urged, his voice low.

I sighed and looked at everyone and figured I knew a lot of their secrets. They might as well know mine. It was just odd to be so near Clay and not touch him. Then Clay reached out and squeezed my knee, and I relaxed marginally. The others smiled or at least looked happy about the touch, so I figured…why the hell not? They all assumed Clay and I were dating anyway. I might as well pretend while living in my own dreams.

"A few of you already know this, but I was married."

Clay nodded, as, of course, Clay and Lee knew, but not everyone else did.

Archer's eyes widened. "How did I not know that?"

"Because you don't need to know everything?" Beckett asked with a grin.

I held back a smile, nearly breaking out in a cold sweat being the center of attention like this. "Anyway, I was married. It didn't work out. I don't want to get into the details, but it didn't work out. My grandmother left me money after she passed, and it wasn't part of the divorce. The way the will was structured, it was clearly and purposely not part of any proceedings that happened with Neil."

"Do you have the paperwork on that?" Jacob asked, tapping his pen.

"Yeah, I do. Though I don't know how it'll help you because you're not my lawyer."

"Pretend with me for a minute," Jacob said as I rolled my eyes.

"Fine. Anyway, Neil wants the bar." I explained in detail what I knew and what was happening on my end. I explained how the divorce had gone, and which paperwork went where.

It didn't make it any easier for me to get it all out there. Contrary to popular belief, I liked my privacy, and I didn't like that I felt as if I were losing something. Then again, maybe that was all on Neil.

"What grounds is he suing you on?" Clay asked. "Because from the way Jacob's frowning, it doesn't seem like he has much of a case."

Jacob snorted. "I don't know exactly what you see on my face, Clay, but honestly, if he's already lost it in the divorce, he shouldn't be able to get your bar. And your lawyers are good."

"They're the best," I teased as Jacob flipped me off.

"I'm trying to help you here, don't make me feel like I'm screwing up."

I ran my hand through my hair and noticed how Clay's gaze went to my forearms. Not the best time for that. "I don't know what I'm supposed to do. I can hand you the paperwork, get you in contact with my lawyers if they want help with this, but it just feels like he's trying to intimidate me." I paused. "And it's fucking working."

Clay reached out and squeezed my hand. The touch made my throat close, and I let out a breath. "We won't let it."

"I don't know about that. Neil's outstanding about messing things up."

"Then we have to be smarter than him," Lee said, setting down his coffee. "First, though, we have cake. Then we'll make some plans. Including bachelor plans because we are here to do a bunch of lists and schedules for the upcoming months while Annabelle is out with the girls."

Jacob crossed his eyes. "I have some ideas for you, Riggs. Let me think on it. As for the rest of the meeting today, let's get through our list. Annabelle will be home and will want to take a nap. The twins are taking a lot out of her."

I leaned forward. "She okay?"

"She is. She's just tired. I don't know how your mother did the whole twin thing twice," Jacob replied with a cringe.

I nodded at him, thinking of the Montgomerys' mother. She'd had five children, two sets of twins. I was drained just thinking about it. "Seriously, I have no idea."

"I'm exhausted with three kids that I didn't have as infants. I don't know how you're going to do it, Jacob," Clay put in.

"You're doing a pretty damn good job," I added softly, ignoring the looks from the others.

"Thanks," he whispered.

Everybody started talking about the bachelor party, my issues tabled for the moment. They wanted to know what was going on, but they wouldn't have answers. I wouldn't either until my lawyers went through everything. It didn't matter that none of us felt that Neil had a case. There was always the potential for catastrophe. Something I had learned far too well.

I looked over at Clay, letting out a breath as I stared into his gorgeous eyes. "Holden doing okay?"

"Yes, doing much better. And, thankfully, as I knock on wood as I say this," Clay said as he literally knocked on the wooden table in front of him, "the other kids didn't get sick."

"Thank God. I was actually really worried about that because I didn't know how you were going to handle it."

Clay shrugged. "I'd handle it."

I believed him. "Good."

We met each other's gazes and didn't say anything until Archer cleared his throat. "Hey, Riggs, Clay is coming to the Montgomery dinner in two nights and bringing the kids. You should come, too."

Marc groaned at his side as everyone spoke up.

"What night?" I asked.

Archer smiled. "Thursday. What do you say?"

"I'm sure you have to work," Clay put in quickly.

"Actually, I don't," I whispered, meeting Clay's eyes, challenging him.

Archer beamed. "See? It's kismet."

The others continued talking about the upcoming bachelor party as I met Clay's gaze. "What are we doing?" Clay whispered.

"I don't know, but it looks like I'm coming to dinner."

Clay sighed and leaned against the back of the couch, but his knee didn't stop touching mine.

This was probably a mistake, something I was good at making. However, why not?

Dating for a single dad and a bar owner meant doing what you could. Whether it was coffee and breakfast with a bunch of guys, a hookup when you could, or a family dinner with a family that wasn't quite yours.

I would have to figure out what I was doing if I wanted this to work. And that was the question. Did I want something more with Clay? Would it blow up in my face as it had with Neil if I tried?

The fact that I was worried that I didn't have the answer to that told me I should be cautious, but the smile on Clay's face as Beckett joked told me that maybe I should just jump.

Just this once.

I'd figure out what to do when I landed.

Chapter 7

Clay

I had been to my fair share of Montgomery family dinners, but this one was my first one bringing a date. Not that I was the one bringing Riggs since Archer had invited him. Nonetheless, here I was, standing in Russell and Pamela Montgomery's living room, surrounded by other Montgomerys, their spouses, their significant others, and my three kids.

I looked over at Riggs, his eyes wide, and we both swallowed hard.

"How did I end up here again?" Riggs asked, and I shook my head.

"I don't know. But I feel like you only have yourself to blame for this one. You could have said you were working."

"Lie to Archer? Have you met the man? He knows all. I'm pretty sure he learned it from his mother." We were talking out of the sides of our mouths. At this point, both of us were trying not to draw attention to each other. As if we were afraid of what would happen if we did.

And, frankly, I *was* afraid. I loved this family. They felt like mine, but they scared me.

Not that they would ever hurt me or shame me or make me feel insignificant, but because they could ferret answers out of an unsuspecting victim even better than the CIA. There was no waterboarding. No, they'd entice you with a cheese plate, and you'd suddenly find yourself sitting next to them, explaining your entire life story as they nodded along and helped you plan your path and enrich your life—all the while setting you up with your dream person. Not that Riggs was my dream person. I couldn't let him be. As I had told him and myself countless times, I did not have time for a dream person.

"Why are you over here sulking?" Paige asked as she came up to us, a frown between her brows.

I swallowed hard and pressed closer to Riggs. He looked down at me and brushed his fingers along mine as his lips quirked into a smile.

"We're not sulking," I corrected, and Paige just smiled.

"Whatever you say. The sooner you come over and talk with my parents, the sooner this will all be over, and you can leave and hide and never come to another Montgomery function again if you don't want to."

The statement was so unlike Paige that both Riggs and I met gazes, confused. She smiled, laughed, and mainly said all the right things, but Paige Montgomery wasn't happy, and I only had an inkling of why.

"Why are you looking at me like that?" Paige asked, her voice low.

I shook my head and pasted a smile on my face. Out of the corner of my eye, I saw Riggs do the same. Look at us, already acting like a couple, even though I wasn't sure what we could call ourselves.

"I came here for the cheese. I'm not quite sure what you're talking about," Riggs replied and winked.

I liked that wink. There was something seriously wrong with me.

"Well, you are at a Montgomery function. There's going to be a lot of cheese. Don't eat too much of it in front of Annabelle, or she will gut you."

"Right, pregnant women can't have soft cheeses?" I asked, wincing.

"Exactly. And she'll hurt you. The same with Brenna."

Paige looked off into the distance. "I'm not even going to eat cheese in front of them just in case. They'll hurt me, and I quite like my face."

"Don't want to have it rearranged?" I asked, teasing.

"I'm off to go eat in private, without Annabelle's gaze. Though she is truly dangerous and probably already knows what I'm doing." She grinned, though it didn't reach her eyes, and then she scampered off.

We stood off to the side, my eagle eye on the kids even as they played with Jacob and the senior Montgomerys. They had some form of wooden block game going that I didn't recognize, but it looked old. Probably a family heirloom.

That made my gut clench because I didn't have those. Not really. You couldn't when your life took drastic and dramatic turns over and over again.

Riggs squeezed my hand, and I looked up at him. "What's wrong?" he asked.

"Just thinking about family. And how things change."

He nodded, his gaze intense and on mine. "I know what you mean. Things change on a dime, especially when you're not expecting it."

"I still can't believe your ex-husband is doing what he is."

"He's an asshole. That's what he does. Honestly, I don't want to talk about him right now. I know I probably should, but my lawyers and Jacob are working on it. It's not going to court. I don't think it can. I'm tired."

"I know all about being tired."

Riggs snorted and looked over at the kids. "I would expect you do."

"I mean, I love them, but they are ridiculous."

"I think they're supposed to be. That's the whole point."

I cleared my throat, remembering a certain conversation I'd had in my newly fixed car. "Anyway, on my way here, Jackson asked me if you and I were dating."

I held back a wince as I said it, as Riggs' eyes widened. "And? What did you tell him?"

"Who said I told him anything?" I asked.

"Because even if you don't have the technical title, you're still their dad. You're not going to lie to them outright."

"And what? Me telling them we're not dating would be a lie?" I asked, leaning forward.

Riggs swallowed hard, and I did my best not to lean any closer. People were watching. Even if it didn't look like it, everybody was always watching. Out of love and care, but we were not alone.

"What did you tell him?" Riggs asked, his voice low.

"I said you were my friend. And we are. So that wasn't a lie."

Disappointment shone in his eyes, and I wanted to reach out and cup his face, though I didn't. Only barely.

"We haven't had a talk yet, so I couldn't tell him more. How was that for an answer?" I asked wryly.

"What are you guys being so serious about over here?" Eliza asked as she walked up, Annabelle and Brenna at her sides.

"Just the normal things," I teased as I hugged Annabelle close. "Shouldn't you'd be sitting?" I looked over at Brenna, the same question in my gaze, and both women rolled their eyes.

"I swear, all of you men, even those without the Montgomery surname, just can't help but be overprotective with me."

"You're pregnant. It's what we do," I replied as I kissed the top of her head.

Riggs beamed. "Seriously, though, you look gorgeous."

Jacob looked across the room, a mock scowl on his face. "Watch it, Riggs. That's my wife you're talking about."

"All I did was call her gorgeous. It's quite clear that she's taken." Riggs winked.

"And you're taken, too," Archer teased.

Benjamin slapped him upside the head playfully. "Really?"

"What? I can't help it. I like to meddle. It's what I do."

"Go meddle in your own drama. Speaking of drama and meddling, where is Marc?" Benjamin asked as he leaned towards Archer.

Archer shrugged, a smile still on his face that didn't look forced, but I wasn't sure. "At work. Emergency meeting. We thought it might happen, so it's not that much of an emergency, more like a well-timed annoyance. Now my RSVP is only one."

"Do you RSVP to Montgomery bashes? Or do you just show up and be welcomed?" I asked, taking the spotlight off Archer. I might not like the attention on me today, but Archer didn't seem to be in the mood, either.

After all, we all had our secrets.

"You know, once a Montgomery, always a Montgomery. And they're always welcome, even if we don't turn on the porch light," the matriarch of the family said as she leaned into her husband's side. "That's what I love about our family. All of our family," she said as she gave her husband a pointed look.

He raised his hands in the air and shook his head. "You're right. We are always welcome at your family's dinner table." He paused. "Just like every Montgomery outside of this house is always welcome here."

I reached out and gripped Riggs' shoulder, telling myself that I wasn't going to cry or make a big deal out of it. Archer's eyes filled as Annabelle legit started crying and leaned into Jacob. Brenna and Eliza gripped hands while Benjamin and Beckett looked at each other and grinned. Riggs gave me a weird look.

"I'll explain later," I whispered, doing my best to make it so no one but him could hear me.

Of course, it seemed I'd forgotten about the kids.

"What's wrong?" Mariah asked as she went to sit in Archer's lap. She patted his cheeks. "Are you okay? Don't cry. I love you." She wrapped her arms around his neck and hugged him tightly as Jackson and Holden went to the girls. They hugged all four women, and everybody started laughing, hugging each other back, a few tears dashed along the way.

I grinned, looked at Riggs, and simply shrugged, not knowing what to say.

Riggs shook his head. "You know, your kids are pretty great."

I smiled. "Yeah, they are."

"I'm glad I'm here. That I was invited."

"I am, too."

Mrs. Montgomery cleared her throat. "Clay, why don't you go show Riggs the new deck we put on last summer break while I get these kids all cleaned up for dinner? Our meal will be served in fifteen minutes."

Everybody scrambled up, and Riggs just beamed, tugging me out to the back porch. "Didn't they already show you the deck?" I asked cautiously.

Riggs rolled his eyes. "Of course, they did. She's giving us time to be alone and being sneaky about it."

I laughed outright. "There's nothing sneaky about what just happened."

"True. But she can't help it. Neither can I."

We stood alone on the corner of the deck where nobody could see us. It was odd, as it felt like I hadn't been alone with Riggs since our night together. My cock pressed against my zipper, and I swallowed hard.

Riggs looked at me with those whiskey-colored eyes and leaned down, brushing a kiss against my lips.

"Hi," he whispered.

I kissed him back softly before I took a step away, needing to breathe. "Hi. It's tough to think with you around. And I cannot get a hard-on in front of the Montgomerys."

Riggs shrugged, adjusting himself. "True. Let's think about something that's not us getting naked."

I raised my brows. "Seriously?"

"What? I can't help it."

"You're an asshole."

"I am, but I'm sure you don't mind. I'm glad that they invited me here. It's nice. Sort of normal in a not-normal sort of way. And there are a lot of people in there."

"Just wait until everybody starts giving birth. Or if any of the other family members show up. It gets a little rowdy."

Riggs looked off into the distance, his shoulder pressing into mine. "I like it, though. I'm just me. You know? I don't have that big family."

My heart hurt for him. I understood his plight all too well. "I think the Montgomerys just adopted you, so you can't say that anymore."

"You know, while I'm a nice friend of the family because of my bar and how the Montgomerys like to come to visit, I think you're the reason I'm here today."

"Yeah?" I asked, my breath getting a little choppy.

"They wanted me here so they could see what's going on between us."

"And? What *is* going on between us, Riggs?" I swallowed hard, my palms going damp.

"Hell if I know. But I think I like it."

I shook my head and laughed. "I have three kids, Riggs. I can't just go off into the unknown."

And that was the crux of it. Why this was a mistake. Only I did not want it to be one.

Riggs studied my face before he seemed to come to a decision. "You're right. I don't know if we can do labels, but if you want, I can make one up for us."

"A label?"

"Whatever you want. However, I like being with you, Clay. I like seeing you smile and trying to make you smile even more. I like your kids, damn it."

My eyes widened. "What?"

"I like your kids. Because one day that little girl of yours is going to rule this world, with Holden at her side, and Jackson as the knight of protection or whatever the hell it's called. They're amazing kids, and I know you're a lot of the reason for that."

I blinked back tears, surprising myself. "You saw all of that. With just one night."

"And today. And every time you talk about them. They're good kids. I know this is complicated, and I know we technically haven't been on a date, yet I feel like you're mine. And I don't know what to do with that."

My heart raced, and I swallowed hard. "That's what I was thinking, but I don't know what happens next or what I should be feeling. I like you, Riggs. You're right. We haven't been on a date."

"We aren't the usual suspects. I work over sixty hours a week most of the time, and you work a full-time job. And those three kids are more than a full-time job. You're making do, and you're doing a kickass job of it. But what would you say if you and I figured out how to date our own way? Not dinner and candlelight, but family barbecues and stolen moments?"

I wanted to. I wanted that so badly. But I didn't know what I was supposed to say. Then Riggs leaned forward and brushed his lips against mine. "You don't have to call yourself my boyfriend. That seems like a big label. But I'd like to see you. At the bar when I'm working, or me coming over for a family dinner one night while the kids are doing homework. We can just hang out and watch a movie when they go to bed. I don't know, Clay. I've never dated someone with a kid before."

"I haven't dated since I got the kids," I blurted.

Riggs' eyes widened. "Seriously? It's been over two years, Clay."

"I know. Tell me about it." I ran my hands through my hair. "You're the first guy since..." I let my voice trail off, and Riggs coughed, realization setting in. I'd been with women in the time since, but Riggs was the only man I'd ever been with. My life was beyond complicated, and things had never worked out. Maybe Riggs had always been in the back of my mind—not that I'd ever let myself think too hard on that.

"Well, then. I'd like to say I'm honored. Though I'd rather be honored a few more times."

I laughed. I couldn't help it. "You're ridiculous."

"I am, but then so are you. And I like you, Clay. I keep telling myself that I have too much baggage, but then you do, too. And what if we help each other carry it? And that's not a euphemism for our dicks."

I burst out laughing and shook my head, falling hard for this man far too quickly for my own good. "So, we date on our terms?"

"Our terms. Whatever that may be. Even if it doesn't always turn out the way we want it to. Let's just figure it out. Because we keep ending up in each other's orbits, and I kind of want to stay."

I swallowed hard, reached out, and finally cupped his face like I wanted to. He leaned into the hold, and then I kissed him softly. "Okay. Let's try. If it gets stirred up, we walk away without hurting each other, with no promises. Because I don't want to hurt you."

"And I don't want to hurt you or those kids. So, we figure it out. You and me."

And then he kissed me again, even as I heard the Montgomerys coming closer. I had to hope that maybe I could actually *have* hope.

For the first time in forever.

Chapter 8

Riggs

I set my phone down before I shook my head and continued making my coffee.

"Are you sure you're up for the soccer game?" Clay asked through the speakerphone, and I grinned, even though he couldn't see me. We were talking as Clay got the kids ready for school, and I was prepping for my day. I had inventory to do and an early delivery, so I'd be heading to the bar soon, while Clay would be heading to the Montgomerys'. It was nice, getting ready in the morning together, even though we were in separate homes and I couldn't see him. Clay was able to put an earbud in his ear so he could talk to me, but video calling wouldn't work while he was running around, making sure that the kids were ready to go.

I still wasn't sure how he did it. However, I was learning.

We'd had nearly two weeks of us doing our version of dating. Meaning not dating or going out. I had dinner at his place and he came into the bar. I hung out with him and the kids and did indeed watch a movie or two while we paid more attention to each other than what was on the screen.

It was nice and nothing like anything I'd ever done in my life.

Except for my marriage to Neil, I had only ever been the hookup guy. Men or women, it didn't matter. I hadn't had the time or the inclination for anything more. And yet, with Clay, that didn't seem to be a problem.

Maybe that should worry me, but it didn't. How could it when I was enjoying myself?

"I'm up for the soccer game. I want to see what that kid can do."

Clay snorted. "He's the sweeper, so he does a lot of running and kicking the ball far."

I grinned. "I was on the soccer team, remember? I know what he does."

Clay cleared his throat. "You were also on the football team and could have done track if spring practice hadn't gotten in the way."

"I tried baseball, too, but I was a little too busy. I was the jock. What can I say?"

"You always did look good in those shorts," Clay mumbled and then cleared his throat as Mariah asked where her shoes were in the background.

I laughed, remembering that Clay had looked damn good in his track shorts, too. Not that I'd been able to see him in them for long. No, we'd had other things to do when we were together.

Clay let out a sigh, and I had to wonder if his mind had gone down the same path as mine. "Anyway. I need to get the kids in, and then I have Montgomery meeting after meeting. Tomorrow is the soccer game. You'd better be there."

"I promised Jackson I'd be there. And you're the one asking if I'm not going to show up, so don't snarl at me."

"I thought you liked it when I snarled."

I grinned, even though he couldn't see me. "True, true. Have fun. I need to head out."

"Have fun doing inventory."

I laughed. "I'm so excited, you don't even know." I took a deep breath, frowned, then said my goodbyes before hanging up, wondering why I'd wanted to add something else to that sentence.

What did you say to the man that was your boyfriend, but you were taking the long, patient way toward a relationship? Not "*I love you.*" Because Clay and I were just getting to know each other again as adults, each with our own baggage. I couldn't love him. Not this soon.

I shook my head, wondering what was wrong with me and made my way towards the bar. I pulled into the rear lot, rolled my shoulders back, and knew today would be a damn fine, good day. I had started the morning off on the phone with someone I knew I could fall for if I wasn't careful, and I was ready. Ready for so fucking much.

I drained the last of my coffee but brought in my travel mug so I could fill it up again and then unlocked the back door. It creaked open, and I frowned, wondering what that smell was.

I took two steps in past the kitchen and looked out into the hallway.

My stomach fell, and my hands shook.

Someone had taken a bat or a two-by-four to the place. The glass picture frames were broken, shattered on the floor. Someone had taken the trash that we hadn't taken out the night before and tore open the bags, tossing the contents all over the place—on top of the tables, the counters, the floor. Someone else—or the same person?—had spray-painted crude words and derogatory things I wasn't even going to think about all over the walls. My hand-carved and patiently stained wood bar top had gouges all over it from what looked like a fucking ax. Tables were upended, chairs were in pieces. I could barely believe what I was seeing.

Everything that I had put into this, my entire *life,* was ruined. Someone had ruined everything, and I didn't understand what I was supposed to do.

I pulled out my phone, wondering if I should call Clay, then shook my head. No, he had things to do.

He had meetings and was probably still dealing with the kids during this time of the morning. I needed to focus. I needed to just... I needed to call the cops. I'd let Clay do his thing and then tell him what happened later. We had a soccer game to go to tomorrow. He had a life. I didn't want to intrude on it.

He had enough on his plate.

As I looked down at the hatred etched onto the walls of the place that was mine, the bar that I had put so much of my soul and creativity into, I knew who had done it. If not with his own hands, then with his bank account. Because Neil was always a petty bitch who got what he wanted. And when he didn't, he took it out on everyone else.

I slipped out of the bar and called the cops, hoping to hell that there were answers out there somewhere. Because I sure as fuck didn't have them.

"Well, it seems your ex is an idiot," Jacob stated as he stood next to me while the cops went over my bar. We were closed. The first time, except for an actual holiday, that Riggs' wouldn't be opening its doors for the neighborhood.

I let out a breath, my body shaking and feeling as if I'd gone three rounds in the ring. "I know he's an idiot, but are you going to tell me why you think he is?"

Jacob sighed. "Because he paid the man who did this with a bank deposit. A straight transfer of funds with a memo. The man they found the fingerprints for."

I blinked and looked up at him. "How the hell do you know this? You're not even a criminal attorney. Do you have like friends on the force or something?"

Jacob laughed. "No, I don't have friends on the force. But I do have a lawyer friend who has friends on the force. They're dealing with Neil now. You're fine."

"Fine. Isn't *fine* a synonym for something being fucked up?"

Jacob sighed. "I'm sorry this happened. Neil fucked up here. He's the one who's going to get in trouble. He paid someone to destroy your bar because he was never going to get what he wanted. I don't know the psychological issues behind that type of response, but he's out of your life forever, Riggs. Some of your place is damaged, yes, but not all of it."

I stuck my hands into my pockets and looked around. My staff had come and gone. I hadn't wanted them to see it, but they had all said that they would be here to help clean up. That they wouldn't leave me.

Insurance would handle most of it, but not everything. My memories, everything that had been put into this place…Neil had taken it.

Just like he had taken so much from me. I hadn't been the same kid I was when I first met him. Right after high school, I had left Clay, even though we hadn't truly been together except for a few stolen moments. I went to college, got my business degree so I could open my bar, and met Neil. I hadn't even graduated yet when Neil got on one knee and I was an idiot and said yes. My grandmother had hated him on sight, but she still loved me. Then, she had gotten a kickass lawyer to make sure Neil never got any of her money.

When she died, and Neil couldn't take not controlling me any longer, I ended up with this place. Today, Neil had tried to take it from me. Forcefully, brutally, and in the fashion he'd become accustomed to.

"He was that much of an idiot?" I asked, rocking back on my heels.

"Yes. Mr. Dumbass didn't think he would be caught because he wasn't the one doing it. He clearly watched too many bad cop shows and didn't realize that the bad guys always get caught."

"Maybe. Fuck, what am I going to do?" It felt overwhelming, and I couldn't keep up.

"You're going to go home, get something to eat, call Clay, and deal with this in the morning. You're not going to be able to go in until the authorities do what they need to do and the insurance company does the appraisal anyway. And then you have the power of the entire Montgomery clan behind you, as well as everybody married into their family—which happens to be a state's worth of people. We'll all help you clean up the place."

I blinked, confused. "What?"

"Don't *what* me. They're going to want to help—all of them. Montgomerys you haven't even met yet have already called Annabelle to set things up. There's a phone tree involved, Riggs."

I blinked, my eyes watering as I fought to keep up with Jacob's words. "What the hell are you talking about?"

"Not only is Riggs' their favorite bar to hang out in, you're family now. And you're dating one of theirs. Clay may not be a Montgomery by name, but he joined the family years ago before he even moved up here. You're his. Therefore, you're theirs."

I didn't know what to think. Everything swirled inside my head, and my hands couldn't stop shaking. Nothing felt real. "Clay and I...we're not ready for anything like that."

"Of course, you're not. But I don't think you're going to have a choice in taking the help offered by his family. My family, too, for that matter."

I kept blinking, wondering how the hell this was my life. "We're not there yet, Jacob. I don't want people putting pressure on him."

"And not you?"

"You married into that family. You get it."

"I do, and I fucked up. More than once. I still feel like I need to grovel every once in a while to show Annabelle I'm sorry for how much of a douche and a dick I was to her. I'm better now. At least, somewhat. And we are going to be parents soon, to twins, and I have no idea what the hell I'm doing. However, I know I'm not going to be alone. Not only do I have the love of my life, I also have her entire support system. It's ridiculous. They're going to help you. *I'm* going to help you. And you've got this. Let the insurance company and authorities do what they need to do. Your other lawyers will work on things for you, and we Montgomerys will be here. Probably with a cheese plate, because that's how we roll."

I shook my head, laughter bubbling up. "I feel like I've been hit by a two-by-four and not my bar. I can't quite keep up."

"Welcome to the Montgomerys. Now, go home. Call Clay. Don't

fuck this up."

I looked at him then. "By *this*, do you mean my bar? Or my relationship with Clay?"

"I said what I said." Then Jacob walked away, and I stood there for a minute longer, wondering what the hell I was going to do.

After I spoke with the authorities a bit more, knowing that there would still be more questions and things to deal with later, I just wanted to go home. Like Jacob had said, I just wanted to be. I hadn't expected the offers of help, but as my phone kept buzzing, the phone tree in full force, I could only shake my head. It seemed I wasn't going to be alone in this. And yet, why did I feel like I was out here all alone?

I headed home, feeling as if I'd run a marathon through wet cement. I walked up to my porch and blinked, my mouth going dry. "Clay?"

Clay stood from where he had been leaning against the side of the door and ran up to me. He threw his arms around me and hugged me tightly. "Are you okay?"

I stood stiff for a moment before I held him close, clinging to him as I let out a shaky breath. "I'm fine. He didn't hurt me."

"He hurt your bar. I know how much you love that place." He cupped my face, then kissed me hard, and I leaned into him, shaking.

"What are you doing here?"

"I'm here for you. Archer's taking the kids. Marc is out of town, but Paige said she would help, so they've got it down. I'm yours for the night."

I blinked at him. "I don't know if you're ready for that," I teased, my emotions all over the place.

He grinned and kissed me again. "Oh, ye of little faith. I think I can handle you. First, you're going to get food in that stomach of yours, and then we're going to talk about what happened." We made our way inside, and Clay pulled out his phone. "I'm ordering us something because I'm not in the mood to cook. I just want to cuddle with you on the couch. You're going to have to deal with it."

"When did you get all bossy?"

"I'm a father of three. It's what I do. Now, sit down."

So, I sat, oddly eager. He did something with his phone, ordered food, and then sat next to me before shoving my head onto his lap so he could play with my hair.

I smiled. "I was expecting something different if you were going to force my head here."

"Maybe later. Talk to me."

And so, I did. I told him about what Jacob had said and what I had seen. How the day had gone. By the end of it, I was shaking again.

Clay tangled the fingers of one hand with mine as he kept his other in my hair, petting me. "That fucker."

I looked up at him, my heart hurting for a whole new reason. This was nice, the two of us. As if we'd done it for far longer than we had. As if it were always meant to be this way. I could love this man. Or maybe I already did. That was scary as hell. "Neil was always an asshole, and he was always an idiot. But I didn't know he was this bad."

Clay's fingers pressed into my scalp, and I nearly purred, my cock hardening. "I'm sorry you went through what you did. And I wish there were something we could do. He's out of your life now. You don't have to deal with him again."

I closed my eyes as I leaned into his touch. "I hope so. But who knows if there's going to be a trial? I don't think I can process that far ahead right now."

"That's something for your lawyers. But they have evidence according to Jacob, so that's a start."

"Neil will no longer be bothering me." I swallowed hard and looked up to meet Clay's gaze. I felt the hard line of his erection below my head but did my best to ignore it. We rarely had time for sex, true, but making time for quiet connection? Almost unheard of.

"Are you okay with that?"

I frowned and sat up to meet his gaze. "What kind of question is that?"

"I have no idea, other than there's something wrong. Talk to me."

I blinked. "I have abysmal taste in men. At least, other than you. Yet here I am with you. And I feel like I'm the bad catch here." I hadn't meant to say that out loud, but here I was, baring myself to the man I thought I could fall in love with.

Clay bent towards me as he stared at my face. "I thought I was the bad bet. The too-busy one, with complications and baggage. We can't both be the bad one."

"I guess I don't know what I'm talking about," I whispered.

"You don't." He let out a breath. "In this moment, it's just you and me. Finally."

I looked up at him before I moved, practically sitting on his lap. "That sounds like a plan to me." I leaned down, and kissed him softly.

It started off gentle, and when the food came, we parted, with Clay picking the food up off the porch and locking the door behind him before sticking it directly in the fridge. My brows lifted, but then I was on my back on the couch again, kissing the man I knew had just made everything better.

It was sweet at first, little nips, soft caresses, and then our shirts were off, and we were rubbing against one another, needing each other's touch. When he slid his hands down the front of my pants, I groaned, loving how he wrapped his hand around my cock.

He stripped off my pants and knelt between my legs on the floor as I sat up on the couch, then he swallowed me whole. I groaned, sliding my fingers through his hair as he went down on me, his mouth so warm and inviting around my dick.

"You're so fucking good at that," I whispered.

"I could get better. I should practice," he teased before humming along my dick, playing with my balls.

I groaned again, tugging at his hair before pulling him up, needing his taste. I stood, pulled off his pants carefully, gripped his dick tightly, and squeezed.

"Jesus," he muttered.

"My name is Riggs. Get used to it." Then I kissed him again, hard.

When I bent him over the couch, I searched in the side table and pulled out condoms and lube.

He looked over his shoulder and laughed. "Really?"

"What? It serves to be prepared. And that's a fucking good couch for what I'm about to do to you."

"I guess so." He laughed, and I fell in love. Again.

Then I kissed him hard before leaving gentle caresses down his back and over his ass. I spread his cheeks before working my fingers inside him, with one hand around him, gripping his cock, the other probing him and getting him ready for me.

We had taken turns the entire time we had been together, and tonight was no different. Because later, after dinner, he would take me, and then we'd fall asleep in a tangle of limbs, and I knew this could be forever. If I got over myself, and we found time, this could be it, but first, I needed to just breathe, and be okay.

And so I worked him harder before I slid the condom over my dick and gently spread him "You ready?"

"Have been forever, fuck me already."

I grinned before I thrust into him with one movement. We both groaned, with Clay letting out a startled laugh.

"Okay, then." His voice was a pant and I nearly came at the guttural groan of it.

"What? You said to fuck you. Now I'm going to." And so I moved, both of us working at a frantic pace as if we were afraid it was going to end too soon. When I reached around and gripped his cock, he put his hand over mine, squeezing harder, and we both moved, coming together in a gasp of ecstasy and passion.

I couldn't believe that this was what my life was now. I couldn't believe that I could finally breathe.

And when we lay on the couch after, both of us shaking, I pulled him close and told myself that tonight could be a beginning if I let myself.

So I held him, and I let the past walk away, if only for the moment.

Chapter 9

Clay

Archer leaned forward over my desk. "I know you can't tell me anything because it's your personal life, but how are you?"

I looked up at the other man and blinked. "Why couldn't I tell you how I am?" I asked, though I had a feeling I knew where Archer was going with this.

Archer just laughed. "I'm trying to be subtle and ask you how you and Riggs are doing." A sad expression covered his face. "I can't believe someone hurt his bar like that. And it was his ex? What a douche."

Anger tore at me, and I let out a deep breath. "I'm so pissed-off. That evil man tried to hurt him."

Archer's eyes widened. "He tried to hurt him? More than the bar?"

I shook my head. "No, I was speaking of emotionally. I mean, his ex-husband did hire someone to destroy the bar. Who knows what else he might have done?" That thought kept me up at night, and I tried not to think about it for long.

Archer reached out and squeezed my hand. "I'm sorry for bringing it up. We're all just so worried about him. Although I hope he knows what he's in for with the cleanup."

I snorted. "I don't think you're talking about the amount of work. I think you're talking about the number of us coming to help."

"Pretty much. The cousins from Denver, Montgomery Inc.—both branches—are on their way. That means we have babysitters for your kids and all the brood they're bringing. And they *are* a brood."

I laughed outright. "I'm pretty sure your family is going to catch up to them in the number of kids it takes to be called a brood."

Archer shrugged. "Sounds like. It's what we do. Although, I don't know when Marc and I are going to have time. Between his job and mine, I'm not sure when we're going to take that next step."

I frowned, doing my best not to cross a line in a potentially sore subject. "Have you guys talked about it? I mean, you *are* getting married."

Archer smiled softly. "Yes, we are getting married. And yes, we've talked about it. While I want kids, and Marc does, too, adoption for us won't be easy. You know?"

I nodded. "We haven't gone through the adoption process. I'm still their guardian, but taking those next steps always felt like something I couldn't do unless all of us were on board and the kids had a say. It's something I've talked about with Jackson, but I'm waiting for the kids to get a little bit older before we make that choice."

Archer grinned. "Good. That's good. You're a great family, and you're a great dad."

I swallowed hard. "It's still scary as hell, though."

"It is, but I guess parenthood should be. As for Marc and me... I don't know. I have plenty of family members I could ask to carry our child, though that's a big ask. Annabelle casually mentioned it when we were teenagers and then again right after her wedding with Jacob. It's our twin thing. Either way, it's a huge and scary thing to even ask."

The love that Archer had for his sister made me smile. The two were close, even as they grew, and I knew Annabelle would do anything for her brother. Much like Archer would do for her. "That's a big step for sure, but your family loves you."

"It's all complicated. Sometimes, I feel like I'd just be a really good uncle."

"You *are* a good uncle. You are to my kids."

Archer beamed. "Well, that's sweet. Now, let's get back to you."

"Get back to what?" I asked.

"How are you feeling?"

"I'm okay. Jackson has a soccer game this afternoon, so we're doing that. And then in a couple of days, Riggs gets the keys back to his bar, and we're going to start the cleanup."

Archer met my gaze and seemed to come to a decision. "I'm going to just outright ask. Are things going good between the two of you?"

I ducked my head, blushing. "Yeah. They are."

Archer squeezed my hand again once before moving away. I looked up and shook my head at his little booty shake.

"What the hell was that for? And please never do that again in my presence."

"Excuse me. I have rhythm. I like the two of you. Especially together. I want everybody to be happy and looking towards the future. That's what happens when you're in love."

"I take it things are going well between you and Riggs, then?" Paige asked as she walked in behind Archer. "Also, Clay is right. Never do that dance again."

"Be nice," Archer teased before kissing her cheek. "I need to head to the meeting. Love you."

"Love you, too," Paige and I said simultaneously, and we both laughed as Archer did another little booty shake out the door.

Paige and I laughed, shaking our heads before she leaned against my desk. "Anyway, I wanted to let you know that I've been making plans and organizing things with Riggs all day to get set up for fixing the bar."

That made me laugh, even as my heart soared. "Really?"

"Of course. The insurance company will be a hassle, but we've got that down. We are good at what we do, so don't you worry. We will organize this wonderfully, and we will make sure that Riggs doesn't have to worry about anything. You're family."

I sighed, a smile on my face. "I guess we are. It still seems weird."

"Well, you're practically a Montgomery now. You have to be used to the weird." She winked. "Have fun at the soccer game tonight. I'm sorry we all can't go. Between meetings and prep for our project, we're all a little bit busy tonight if we want to get in time working at Riggs'."

I leaned back in my chair, work hard to focus on just then. "I still can't believe you guys usually come to the games."

"Of course, we do. We need to cheer on our next generation. We love those kids, Clay. We're a family operation, even if our family is a little convoluted. Now, I'll let you get back to work. Later, you can tell me all about Riggs. The man, not the bar." She winked as she said it, sounding like her old self, and I shook my head, holding back a laugh as she left.

Everybody was so invested in my relationship. And yet, *I* didn't know what was going to happen. I was falling head over heels in love with Riggs. And, honestly, I was terrified that it was too soon. That it would be too much and he'd walk away. But then would he? He had stayed so far, and while we had done a good job of trying to push each other away, we hadn't yet. That had to count for something, didn't it?

I shook my head and got back to work since Beckett expected a few things from me. There would be time for Riggs and my thoughts on him later. Because in the end, I would make that time. Finally.

By the time I was done and did the normal after-school routine, I was already a little wired and yet exhausted at the same time.

Riggs showed up as I was getting Jackson ready for his game and kissed me softly on the mouth, pushing my hair back from my face. "You ready?"

"For what?" I asked.

Riggs laughed. "That's what I thought."

"Riggs!" Mariah cheered as she ran to him. She jumped about two feet away from him and flew in the air. That little girl was ready for gymnastics and was already doing fantastic at her tumbling class. Only it was still a little startling to see her jump like that.

Riggs caught her with ease, my heart racing, and spun her around the living room. Holden was there, hugging Riggs on the side as the man I loved lifted Mariah to his hip.

"I see we're ready to go."

"We want to see Jackson kick ass!" Mariah called out, and Riggs pressed his lips together, doing his best not to laugh.

I leaned toward my kid. "What did we say about that word, Mariah?"

"That ass is a donkey."

Holden began to laugh as Jackson came out holding his cleats, his shin guards in place. I didn't let him wear his cleats in the house as they tended to get caught in the carpet, so he usually put them on once we got to the fields. He had on his tennis shoes for now, and that would have to do.

Jackson gave a put-upon sigh. "Don't say that, please. They think it's cute now, and then you're not a little kid anymore, and they get all angry when you use those words."

I narrowed my eyes at my oldest. "Really? That's what you're going with?"

Jackson shrugged, the light in his eyes dancing. "What? It's the truth."

"Perhaps. Now, let's get going. Do you have your water?"

"Yes!" all three kids said at the same time.

Riggs grinned. "I have my water, too. We're taking your car, right?"

"Yep. You're piling in with us."

"And you can sit with me," Mariah whispered. She patted his cheek and looked like she had fallen in love with him.

Same here, little girl.

"He's going to want to sit next to Clay," Holden said.

"Duh," Jackson added. "They're boyfriends."

"Well, he can be my boyfriend, too," Mariah added, and I froze. We hadn't talked to the kids about exactly what was going on between Riggs and me, mostly because that would entail Riggs and I talking about what was going on between us.

I cleared my throat. "Mariah."

"No, I got this," Riggs said and looked between the kids. "Yep, I'm dating Clay. So that means you're stuck with me. Sorry. However, you'll have to help me figure out how to be this boyfriend of a dad thing. Okay?"

"Clay's the best dad," Mariah added, her smile sweet. I swallowed hard at her words, trying not to cry.

"He is the best," Holden added, and Jackson nodded.

My eldest smiled. "We usually call him Clay. Because he was Clay before, and we like it. Plus, other kids don't get to call their dads by their first name. So, we're special."

I held back a laugh at that, wondering how I'd gotten so lucky, even when I didn't always feel it. "Okay, then. I guess we should go."

"You can sleep in his bed if you want," Mariah put in as we loaded the SUV.

Riggs tripped over his feet, keeping his hold on her. "What?" he asked, his voice high-pitched.

"My friend Kathy's mom has her boyfriends sleep over. Just one at a time. I don't think the guys know about each other, though, because it's all very secretive. It's fine because we're keeping the secret."

Riggs looked ready to burst, and I couldn't meet his gaze, or I would laugh outright. Thankfully, Jackson and Holden didn't truly understand what was going on, and I counted that as a win because...dear God.

We piled into my car, and Riggs leaned across the center console to kiss me. I froze, as we didn't usually do this in front of the kids. Mariah just clapped, and Holden and Jackson smiled widely so I went with it.

"Hi," Riggs said.

"Hi," I added. "I guess we're doing this."

"Okay, I guess so."

Then I pulled out of the driveway and headed to the soccer game for my kids, my boyfriend right beside me.

"Go, Jackson!" Riggs called out, clapping his hands. He paced the sidelines along with Holden, my middle child echoing every gesture Riggs made.

It was adorable, and I had already taken a couple of photos. I couldn't help it. My kids were falling for my boyfriend. And it was one of the best moments of my life.

I sat with Mariah on my lap as she watched the game. She had been sitting next to me before but decided that she liked seeing better from my vantage point. When Riggs and Holden came back, I leaned into my boyfriend and smiled.

"Have fun?"

Riggs grinned. "Yeah. Having a lot of fun."

"I still can't believe you're here."

"Got to be here for my man, Jackson."

And that was it. I loved him. There was no turning back now. We focused on the game, cheering for Jackson as he came out.

Then everything happened all at once.

A bigger kid pummeled Jackson, tripping him. The ref already had his red card in hand, but I was on my feet in an instant, running to the field despite the other parents' warnings. I had handed Mariah to Riggs, knowing without words that he would keep my kids safe as I ran to my eldest on the ground.

The coaches were there as Jackson held his arm.

"It hurts," Jackson whined, clearly trying not to cry.

I fell to my knees, cupping his little face. "It's okay, buddy. We've got you."

Riggs was behind me, keeping both kids a little bit away, and I met his gaze. Fear crashed into me, but I told myself that this was okay.

Everything would be okay.

It had to be.

Another hospital and ER visit later, Jackson was diagnosed with a hairline fracture in his radius but would be fine soon. Children healed quickly, and the break wasn't that bad, but it still hurt.

While they got Jackson set up to go home, I figured I could leave him alone for just a moment, knowing he would be fine. I kissed the top of his head but stopped on my way out the door so I could head to the waiting area. "What can I get you?"

"I'm good. Say hi to Riggs. And tell the others I'm okay. I know Mariah was scared."

"You're a pretty great kid, Jackson," I said, swallowing the lump in my throat.

"Yeah, I try. Love you, Dad."

I swallowed hard and then walked on wobbly legs as tears threatened.

Riggs gave my face one look and ran to me after telling Holden to watch Mariah. "What's wrong?" he asked, cupping my face.

"Jackson just called me Dad."

Riggs blinked. "Wow. That's something."

"Don't know if he'll do it always. He doesn't have to. Hell."

"Hell," Riggs repeated, a slow smile spreading across his face.

"I can't believe you're here," I whispered.

"Of course, I am. Jackson got hurt. I love those kids, Clay." He swallowed hard. "And I love you."

This time, the tears did fall. I leaned forward and kissed him softly. There were only a couple of people in the emergency room, and they weren't paying any attention to us. We could still have eyes on Mariah and Holden, but I stood there, needing to breathe. "I love you, too, Riggs. It scares me. In the best way possible."

Riggs winked. "We've got this."

"Okay. We do. Wow."

Riggs grinned and then looked over at Mariah and Holden. "Are we taking Jackson home soon?"

I shook out my worries and bubbles of emotion over what'd just happened, telling myself to get in the game. "He'll be fine. We are taking him home in a minute. I'm going to go get him now."

"Yay," Mariah said. "I don't like him hurt."

"Same here," Riggs said as he picked up Mariah again and set her on his hip. He was getting good at that. "How about we clean up our mess over in that corner and get ready for them?" Riggs said. "That way, we can get Jackson and be ready to go home."

"Okay," Holden said, rocking back on his heels. "I wasn't scared."

I looked at Holden, nodding. "Really?"

"No. Because you were there for him, and then Riggs was here for us. It's like we're a family." He shrugged and then walked away as if he hadn't just dropped that bombshell.

Riggs met my gaze, but there wasn't any fear in his eyes. Instead, I saw a sense of purpose as he leaned down, kissed me again, then pushed me towards the double doors. "Go get our boy. I've got the others."

And he did. I trusted him.

I had fallen in love with my high school crush, and I hadn't meant to.

I had told myself that I didn't have time for love or anyone else, but it seemed fate had time for me.

Epilogue

Riggs

A month later.

If you asked the Montgomerys to help you begin a small country as the next steppingstone towards world domination, I was pretty sure all you needed to offer was beer and cheese and maybe a friendly game of poker, and they would get it done in less than a month.

The bar was mine. Riggs' was all mine. I had been self-centered enough to name it after myself because my grandmother had always liked my name, but Neil wouldn't have an inch of it.

I wasn't sure what would happen to Neil legally. They had all the evidence that he had taken out a hit on my bar, and they had the man who had done it, who had entered into a plea deal in exchange for information about Neil.

I wasn't sure what would happen. I just knew that I had nothing to do with it. The bar was mine, and my ex-husband was so out of my life, he was barely even a memory. Tonight was time for a party.

The out-of-town Montgomerys had all headed home, taking their brood and all their help with them. The Fort Collins Montgomerys, however, were here for me. The bar would reopen full-time again tomorrow as a lot of the community had come to help and ensure that I wouldn't have to close the doors forever.

As soon as I was legally able to start serving drinks and food again, I had reopened, even when not all of the repairs were complete. The regulars had come in droves in a show of support, and I knew that while the bubble wouldn't last, I still felt like people loved being there.

That they liked me.

I couldn't believe it.

I looked over at the Montgomerys as they partied and danced, though Jacob and Annabelle weren't here since they were home with newborn twins. Paige wasn't here either, but I wasn't going to ask why. Archer was here, dancing with Eliza and Brenna, and the others milled about, having a good time.

I only had eyes for Clay.

"The kids okay with the sitter?"

Clay grinned at me. "Yeah. They miss their Riggs, though. I swear you've become number one in their life. Seems I was easy to walk over."

I rolled my eyes and leaned forward, kissing him softly on the mouth. Archer cheered, and I ignored him. "Your kids are pretty amazing."

"Jackson's back to calling me Clay, but it's kind of nice that he called me Dad that once."

"He might do it again. Just let it happen."

"I know." He swallowed hard and met my gaze. "I love you so much, Riggs. I didn't expect you."

"I'm the best unexpected." I winked, loving how I made him laugh. "And I love you, too. Now, come dance with me."

"You know, the last time we danced, it led to something more."

"Why do you think I'm asking you?" I asked, waggling my brows. Clay threw back his head and laughed, looking sexy as fuck. I pulled him into my arms as we danced. It was just a small party to get ready for the grand reopening tomorrow, but all I could do was focus on the man in my arms, the one I hadn't planned on.

"We're taking the kids out for an early dinner tomorrow, right?" I asked, knowing that I would be busy beyond all measure in the next few weeks, but I didn't want to miss out on any of the kids' milestones or time with Clay.

"You've got it. You sure they're okay coming in here?"

"For lunch or an early dinner? The kids are welcome. It's at night when things get rowdy that they're not."

"I don't know if you're trying to have a euphemism there or not," Clay added dryly before I kissed him. I couldn't focus on anything else, just the man in my arms. I had been crushing on him hard for what felt like forever, remembering the boys we used to be when we had thought we could have something more. And when life and our decisions took that from us, I hadn't thought I would get a second chance.

But here I was, with that second chance and the man I loved.

We were going to take things as slow as we possibly could, mostly so we didn't scare the kids. It was one thing having me over every once in a while. It was quite another to have me moving in or putting a ring on that finger.

I would, though. This man would be my husband, and I would have to figure out exactly how to help Clay raise those three pretty fantastic kids. That time would come.

For now, it was just us and nothing else.

"I've decided to get the Montgomery tattoo," Clay muttered.

I gazed into his eyes, grinning. "Really?"

"It was Paige's idea. And while I've always wanted one, I also wanted to make her smile."

I rolled my eyes. "You're getting a tattoo to make a woman smile?"

"What? They keep telling me I've been adopted into the family. And I've been part of the Montgomerys for nearly my entire life now. I guess it's time I make it official."

I shook my head, though not surprised. "Where are you going to put it?"

"I was thinking somewhere in the ink on my shoulder."

I nodded, thinking about the intricate piece he'd had done before he moved here. I enjoyed licking every inch of it. "I'll help you baby it to healing. Don't worry. I've got you."

"That sounds like a plan."

"I guess if you're a Montgomery, that means I'm dating into the family. That's a little scary."

"Be scared. It's sort of what they do." He kissed me hard, and I danced with him, joining the others as a faster song came on. I leaned into the love of my life, standing in the bar that was a culmination of so many of my dreams, and just grinned.

I hadn't expected any of this, and yet, it was what I needed.

My friends, my family, and my future.

I didn't need anything else. Finally.

* * * *

Also from 1001 Dark Nights and Carrie Ann Ryan, discover Captured in Ink, Taken With You, Ashes to Ink, Inked Nights, Hidden Ink, Adoring Ink, and Wicked Wolf

Sign up for the 1001 Dark Nights Newsletter
and be entered to win a Tiffany Key necklace.

There's a contest every month!

Go to www.1001DarkNights. com to subscribe.

**As a bonus, all subscribers can download
FIVE FREE exclusive books!**

Discover 1001 Dark Nights Collection Nine

DRAGON UNBOUND by Donna Grant
A Dark Kings Novella

NOTHING BUT INK by Carrie Ann Ryan
A Montgomery Ink: Fort Collins Novella

THE MASTERMIND by Dylan Allen
A Rivers Wilde Novella

JUST ONE WISH by Carly Phillips
A Kingston Family Novella

BEHIND CLOSED DOORS by Skye Warren
A Rochester Novella

GOSSAMER IN THE DARKNESS by Kristen Ashley
A Fantasyland Novella

THE CLOSE-UP by Kennedy Ryan
A Hollywood Renaissance Novella

DELIGHTED by Lexi Blake
A Masters and Mercenaries Novella

THE GRAVESIDE BAR AND GRILL by Darynda Jones
A Charley Davidson Novella

THE ANTI-FAN AND THE IDOL by Rachel Van Dyken
A My Summer In Seoul Novella

A VAMPIRE'S KISS by Rebecca Zanetti
A Dark Protectors/Rebels Novella

CHARMED BY YOU by J. Kenner
A Stark Security Novella

HIDE AND SEEK by Laura Kaye
A Blasphemy Novella

DESCEND TO DARKNESS by Heather Graham
A Krewe of Hunters Novella

BOND OF PASSION by Larissa Ione
A Demonica Novella

JUST WHAT I NEEDED by Kylie Scott
A Stage Dive Novella

Also from Blue Box Press

THE BAIT by C.W. Gortner and M.J. Rose

THE FASHION ORPHANS by Randy Susan Meyers and M.J. Rose

TAKING THE LEAP by Kristen Ashley
A River Rain Novel

SAPPHIRE SUNSET by Christopher Rice writing C. Travis Rice
A Sapphire Cove Novel

THE WAR OF TWO QUEENS by Jennifer L. Armentrout
A Blood and Ash Novel

THE MURDERS AT FLEAT HOUSE BY Lucinda Riley

THE HEIST by C.W. Gortner and M.J. Rose

Discover More Carrie Ann Ryan

Captured in Ink
A Montgomery Ink: Boulder Novella

Julia and Ronin know their relationship is solid. They've been through hell and back, but their love has stayed true through it all. When Ronin's ex, Kincaid, comes back to town, however, the two realize what they might be missing.

Kincaid didn't mean to leave Ronin behind all those years ago. When tragedy struck not once, but twice, bringing with it the heat of horror, he couldn't face the past he'd left behind. Now, he's back and doesn't know how he fits in with the seemingly perfect couple—especially not when their families will apparently stop at nothing to keep them apart.

* * * *

Taken With You
A Fractured Connections Novella

It all started at a wedding. Beckham didn't mean to dance with Meadow. And he really didn't mean to kiss her. But now, she's the only thing on his mind. And when it all comes down to it, she's the only person he can't have.

He'll just have to stay away from her, no matter how hard they're pulled together.

Running away from her friend's wedding isn't the best way to keep the gossip at bay. But falling for the mysterious and gorgeous bartender at her friends' bar will only make it worse. Beckham has his secrets, and she refuses to pry.

Once burned, twice kicked down, and never allowed to get up again. Yet taking a chance with him might be the only choice she has. And the only one she wants.

**For fans of Carrie Ann's Fractured Connections series, Taken With You is book four in that series.

* * * * *

Ashes to Ink
A Montgomery Ink: Colorado Springs Novella

Back in Denver, Abby lost everything she ever loved, except for her daughter, the one memory she has left of the man she loved and lost. Now, she's moved next to the Montgomerys in Colorado Springs, leaving her past behind to start her new life.

One step at a time.

Ryan is the newest tattoo artist at Montgomery Ink Too and knows the others are curious about his secrets. But he's not ready to tell them. Not yet. That is...until he meets Abby.

Abby and Ryan thought they had their own paths, ones that had nothing to do with one another. Then...they took a chance.

On each other.

One night at a time.

* * * *

Inked Nights
A Montgomery Ink Novella

Tattoo artist, Derek Hawkins knows the rules:
  One night a month.
  No last names.
  No promises.

Olivia Madison has her own rules:
  Don't fall in love.
  No commitment.
  Never tell Derek the truth.

When their worlds crash into each other however, Derek and Olivia will have to face what they fought to ignore as well as the connection they tried to forget.

* * * *

Adoring Ink
A Montgomery Ink Novella

Holly Rose fell in love with a Montgomery, but left him when he couldn't love her back. She might have been the one to break the ties and ensure her ex's happy ending, but now Holly's afraid she's missed out on more than a chance at forever. Though she's always been the dependable good girl, she's ready to take a leap of faith and embark on the journey of a lifetime.

Brody Deacon loves ink, women, fast cars, and living life like there's no tomorrow. The thing is, he doesn't know if he *has* a tomorrow at all. When he sees Holly, he's not only intrigued, he also hears the warnings of danger in his head. She's too sweet, too innocent, and way too special for him. But when Holly asks him to help her grab the bull by the horns, he can't help but go all in.

As they explore Holly's bucket list and their own desires, Brody will have to make sure he doesn't fall too hard and too fast. Sometimes, people think happily ever afters don't happen for everyone, and Brody will have to face his demons and tell Holly the truth of what it means to truly live life to the fullest…even when they're both running out of time.

* * * *

Hidden Ink
A Montgomery Ink Novella

The Montgomery Ink series continues with the long-awaited romance between the café owner next door and the tattoo artist who's loved her from afar.

Hailey Monroe knows the world isn't always fair, but she's picked herself up from the ashes once before and if she needs to, she'll do it again. It's been years since she first spotted the tattoo artist with a scowl that made her heart skip a beat, but now she's finally gained the courage to approach him. Only it won't be about what their future could bring, but how to finish healing the scars from her past.

Sloane Gordon lived through the worst kinds of hell yet the temptation next door sends him to another level. He's kept his distance because he knows what kind of man he is versus what kind of man Hailey needs. When she comes to him with a proposition that sends his mind whirling and his soul shattering, he'll do everything in his power to protect the woman he cares for and the secrets he's been forced to keep.

* * * *

Wicked Wolf
A Redwood Pack Novella

The war between the Redwood Pack and the Centrals is one of wolf legend. Gina Eaton lost both of her parents when a member of their Pack betrayed them. Adopted by the Alpha of the Pack as a child, Gina grew up within the royal family to become an enforcer and protector of her den. She's always known fate can be a tricky and deceitful entity, but when she finds the one man that could be her mate, she might throw caution to the wind and follow the path set out for her, rather than forging one of her own.

Quinn Weston's mate walked out on him five years ago, severing their bond in the most brutal fashion. She not only left him a shattered shadow of himself, but their newborn son as well. Now, as the lieutenant of the Talon Pack's Alpha, he puts his whole being into two things: the safety of his Pack and his son.

When the two Alphas put Gina and Quinn together to find a way to ensure their treaties remain strong, fate has a plan of its own. Neither knows what will come of the Pack's alliance, let alone one between the two of them. The past paved their paths in blood and heartache, but it will take the strength of a promise and iron will to find their future.

An excerpt from Captured in Ink by Carrie Ann Ryan

I smiled over at Julia again as Ethan began talking about work and an upcoming trip, and I wondered when we would start that next phase of our relationship. We both wanted children and had talked about it in the past, but we were taking our time. We still had more to do in our lives before we took that next step, but it would probably be a good idea to at least bring it up so we were on the same page.

I had learned long ago from one disastrous relationship after another that without true communication, things could get fucked up faster than you could blink. And I would do everything in my power to never hurt Julia.

"You're not going on this work trip?" I asked Ethan, trying to get my head back into the conversation.

Both Julia and Ethan were computational chemists, with Julia focused on data analysis. However, she worked with Ethan on most projects. Both of them were way above my pay grade when it came to understanding science, but I liked learning new things. Hence why, after I left the military, I became a librarian, something the exact opposite of what my initial career had been. Some people might not quite understand why, but it was books for me, and that's all I needed. That, and Julia.

"No, they only need Julia and another member of our team. I offered to go in her place because I know you have an anniversary coming up, but she's the one who spearheaded this, you know?" Ethan added.

Julia just shook her head. "We did it together, thank you very much. You were just as big a part of this project as I was. But you know Jeff, he wanted to go because the event is in Vegas, so it was either you or me and the guy in charge."

I ground my teeth. "I don't like this Jeff guy."

Julia shrugged. "He's not that bad. He's brilliant, and he's always quite nice. And he isn't one of those guys who thinks that because I'm a woman, I don't know how to do science or come up with my own proofs. But he's also in a higher position than us, and if he wants to go on a trip where he will get his work done but also party? He's going to go."

"Yeah, he's not a jerk," Ethan put in. "And he did do work on the project. So, it's not like there's any bad blood."

"I still don't have to like him," I said, lifting my chin.

Julia just snorted. "Of course not, honey. You can hate him all you want."

"I heard that placating tone," I said dryly.

"It wasn't like I was hiding it."

"You two are way too cute." Holland smiled broadly as she looked between us.

I grinned. "Thank you. We try."

About Carrie Ann Ryan

Carrie Ann Ryan is the *New York Times* and USA Today bestselling author of contemporary, paranormal, and young adult romance. Her works include the Montgomery Ink, Talon Pack, Promise Me, and Elements of Five series, which have sold millions of books worldwide. She's the winner of a RT Book of the Year and a Prism Award in her genres. She started writing while in graduate school for her advanced degree in chemistry and hasn't stopped since. Carrie Ann has written over seventy-five novels and novellas with more in the works. When she's not losing herself in her emotional and action-packed worlds, she's reading as much as she can while wrangling her clowder of cats who have more followers than she does.

www.CarrieAnnRyan.com

Discover 1001 Dark Nights

ABANDON by Rachel Van Dyken ~ THE OPEN DOOR by Laurelin Paige ~ CLOSER by Kylie Scott ~ SOMETHING JUST LIKE THIS by Jennifer Probst ~ BLOOD NIGHT by Heather Graham ~ TWIST OF FATE by Jill Shalvis ~ MORE THAN PLEASURE YOU by Shayla Black ~ WONDER WITH ME by Kristen Proby ~ THE DARKEST ASSASSIN by Gena Showalter

COLLECTION SEVEN
THE BISHOP by Skye Warren ~ TAKEN WITH YOU by Carrie Ann Ryan ~ DRAGON LOST by Donna Grant ~ SEXY LOVE by Carly Phillips ~ PROVOKE by Rachel Van Dyken ~ RAFE by Sawyer Bennett ~ THE NAUGHTY PRINCESS by Claire Contreras ~ THE GRAVEYARD SHIFT by Darynda Jones ~ CHARMED by Lexi Blake ~ SACRIFICE OF DARKNESS by Alexandra Ivy ~ THE QUEEN by Jen Armentrout ~ BEGIN AGAIN by Jennifer Probst ~ VIXEN by Rebecca Zanetti ~ SLASH by Laurelin Paige ~ THE DEAD HEAT OF SUMMER by Heather Graham ~ WILD FIRE by Kristen Ashley ~ MORE THAN PROTECT YOU by Shayla Black ~ LOVE SONG by Kylie Scott ~ CHERISH ME by J. Kenner ~ SHINE WITH ME by Kristen Proby

COLLECTION EIGHT
DRAGON REVEALED by Donna Grant ~ CAPTURED IN INK by Carrie Ann Ryan ~ SECURING JANE by Susan Stoker ~ WILD WIND by Kristen Ashley ~ DARE TO TEASE by Carly Phillips ~ VAMPIRE by Rebecca Zanetti ~ MAFIA KING by Rachel Van Dyken ~ THE GRAVEDIGGER'S SON by Darynda Jones ~ FINALE by Skye Warren ~ MEMORIES OF YOU by J. Kenner ~ SLAYED BY DARKNESS by Alexandra Ivy ~ TREASURED by Lexi Blake ~ THE DAREDEVIL by Dylan Allen ~ BOND OF DESTINY by Larissa Ione ~ MORE THAN POSSESS YOU by Shayla Black ~ HAUNTED HOUSE by Heather Graham ~ MAN FOR ME by Laurelin Paige ~ THE RHYTHM METHOD by Kylie Scott ~ JONAH BENNETT by Tijan ~ CHANGE WITH ME by Kristen Proby ~ THE DARKEST DESTINY by Gena Showalter

Discover Blue Box Press
TAME ME by J. Kenner ~ TEMPT ME by J. Kenner ~ DAMIEN by J. Kenner ~ TEASE ME by J. Kenner ~ REAPER by Larissa Ione ~ THE

SURRENDER GATE by Christopher Rice ~ SERVICING THE TARGET by Cherise Sinclair ~ THE LAKE OF LEARNING by Steve Berry and M.J. Rose ~ THE MUSEUM OF MYSTERIES by Steve Berry and M.J. Rose ~ TEASE ME by J. Kenner ~ FROM BLOOD AND ASH by Jennifer L. Armentrout ~ QUEEN MOVE by Kennedy Ryan ~ THE HOUSE OF LONG AGO by Steve Berry and M.J. Rose ~ THE BUTTERFLY ROOM by Lucinda Riley ~ A KINGDOM OF FLESH AND FIRE by Jennifer L. Armentrout ~ THE LAST TIARA by M.J. Rose ~ THE CROWN OF GILDED BONES by Jennifer L. Armentrout ~ THE MISSING SISTER by Lucinda Riley ~ THE END OF FOREVER by Steve Berry and M.J. Rose ~ THE STEAL by C. W. Gortner and M.J. Rose ~ CHASING SERENITY by Kristen Ashley ~ A SHADOW IN THE EMBER by Jennifer L. Armentrout

On Behalf of 1001 Dark Nights,

Liz Berry, M.J. Rose, and Jillian Stein would like to thank ~

Steve Berry
Doug Scofield
Benjamin Stein
Kim Guidroz
Social Butterfly PR
Ashley Wells
Asha Hossain
Chris Graham
Chelle Olson
Kasi Alexander
Jessica Saunders
Dylan Stockton
Kate Boggs
Richard Blake
and Simon Lipskar

Made in United States
North Haven, CT
24 January 2022

15226079R00071